TIMBERLAND REGIONAL LIBRARY
P9-CKX-414
A20011

HAPHAZARD HOUSE

HAPHAZARD HOUSE

Mary Wesley

THE OVERLOOK PRESS
WOODSTOCK • NEW YORK

First published in 1993 by
The Overlook Press
Lewis Hollow Road
Woodstock, New York 12498

Library of Congress Cataloging-in-Publication Data

Wesley, Mary
Haphazard House / Mary Wesley
p. cm.
Summary: Eleven-year-old Lisa and her family meet the future when they enter a time warp.

[1. Time travel–Fiction. 2. Family life–Fiction.] I. Title.

PZ7.W5Hap 1993
[Fic]—dc20

ISBN : 0-87951-470-1

92-24590
CIP
AC

'Life is a stair up which Death beckons.'
Anonymous

Chapter 1

Josh and I sat at the top of the stairs listening to the voices below.

'You were very keen when he suggested it in the first place.' Our mother had said this several times.

'Well, I'm not keen now. The whole thing is idiotic, pretentious, and a waste of my time. I shall not go; it might kill me.'

'Josh and I enjoyed ourselves.'

'I don't approve.'

'Darling, Sandy knows what he is doing; he's a very good agent. You'd see if you'd take the trouble to go.' Our mother's voice rose. Josh put his head on one side and began to conduct an imaginary orchestra, a Biro in his right hand, his left outstretched with fingers spread.

'Sandy just wants to make money.'

'Some money would be nice.' Ma's voice dropped a note.

'Money, money, money.' Josh waggled the Biro.

'Next you'll say that's all I think about!' Her voice rose, suddenly harsh. Josh threw up his arms, holding them stiff.

'Oh, don't let's quarrel.' The key was low. 'You know my principles.'

'I'm not quarrelling. I just think you should go.'

'I'd be recognized.'

'Why not?'

'People would ask silly questions.'

'Rot.'

'You know they would. It's a racket, a racket, a racket.' Josh emphatically waved the Biro.

'It's Sandy's job. The pictures are beautifully framed, you said so yourself; and they are well hung. Do go.'

'I won't.'

'You must.'

'Why should I?'

'Out of common politeness.'

'Politeness!' Very low growling. 'Rallentando,' murmured Josh.

'No. No. No.'

'Presto,' whispered Josh.

'Darling—please go. Take Lisa. She only didn't come with me because of you.'

'Very sensible child.' Josh raised an eyebrow.

'For your father's sake then.'

'How does he come into it?'

'He's old; he hasn't got much longer.'

'I know that.'

'It would give him a boost; make him proud to see your success.'

'What success?'

'A one-man show is success.'

'Not if it's a flop.'

'It won't be a flop. Go for his sake. Let him see your success before he dies.'

'We are all dying.'

'He is nearer to it than you. He's a lonely old man.'

'He doesn't believe in my painting; he scoffs.' Josh held the Biro still. I held my breath.

'He lives in peril of eviction.'

'He's been in peril of eviction ever since he moved into that flat when my mother died.'

'It's much worse now, and he's that much older. Please go.'

'The Council will find him somewhere.'

'It won't be the same and he won't be allowed to keep a cat.'

'What has my father's cat got to do with the exhibition of my paintings?'

'Oh! You are exasperating! I could massacre you!'

Josh waved the Biro and clenched his left fist.

'You can only massacre a lot of people. I am alone.'

'She's winning,' I whispered.

'Never mind my grammar!' Ma was furious.

'I love your grammar. I love you. I love our horrible children.'

'Oh, darling—'

'I hate exhibitions. I hate commerce. I hate living here. I just want peace to paint.'

'Then you'll go?'

'All right.' Very quiet, muted.

'Good. I've found a suit at a jumble sale you can wear. Nobody will know you.'

'A suit!' Pa's voice sounded like a runaway trumpet blast. 'I never wear suits.'

'That's why it's so perfect. You can see for yourself how well the pictures have been hung. I shall make Lisa presentable, too.'

They burst out laughing. Josh brought the concert to a close. I mimed clapping hands.

'*How* stupid articulate adults can sound!' Josh grinned.

'I want to go, really,' I said as I got up from the stairs.

'Of course you do.'

'Do people make remarks?'

'Nothing nasty. I was surprised how good it was. He makes out he's not marvellous but other people—'

'What?'

'You go and see. Goodnight.' Josh went off to bed.

In the morning Pa looked clean and tidy and I did, too. Ma had achieved the impossible; Pa looked ordinary, like other people. He still stood very tall, six-foot-four but, in a pepper-and-salt suit, polished shoes and blue socks, he might have passed for anyone other than an unknown painter going to see his first one-man show in London.

'A hat?' Pa suggested timidly.

'No. They are not worn except by parsons and people like that.'

'Who are like parsons?'

'Don't be difficult; you know what I mean. Lawyers, parsons, etc.'

Pa shut up.

Ma looked at me, her eyes travelling from my well-brushed head to my feet in school shoes. She suppressed a smile.

'Nobody will know you.'

'Sure?'

'Absolutely.'

Ma and Josh stood in the doorway and watched us get into the beat-up Mini—for Pa an athletic feat. When driving, the curious would turn and stare as his head touched the roof and, even with the seat as far back as it would go, his legs had to be folded so that they did not get in the way of the driving wheel.

'Off we go then,' he cried. I waved. Ma and Josh waved. Pa drove down the road and headed for inner London. Ma had told me to keep Pa happy and calm.

'Ma says nobody paid any attention to her or Josh and that no one said anything derogatory.'

'Derogatory?'

'Unsuited to your dignity.'

'What dignity?'

'You look very dignified in that rig.'

'Ah, Lisa, I am glad to have you with me. Perhaps if I got a hat people would just think I was some country parson up for the day with his little girl having a dekko at modern art on the way to the dentist.'

'Ma said no hat, and I *am* on the way to the dentist.'

'I know. I can't think why you and Josh make such a fuss; neither of you has ever been hurt.'

'We will be one day. Perhaps today is that day for me.'

'Lisa, I'm sure your mother told you to keep me calm and cheerful. This is no way to set about it. Let us plan,' said Pa, reversing our roles and making an effort to console me for the visit to the dentist which lay ahead. 'Let us plan what to do with the money if I have sold a picture or two. Let's be wildly optimistic.'

'I should think you'd like to put it on a horse.'

'What would your mother say?'

'We needn't tell her if it doesn't win.'

'Isn't that a bit, er, dishonest or something? It's against her principles, is betting '

'She wants a Hoover or a colour television.'

'Well, that's against my principles, as you well know. I am against gadgets, and television in particular. The money on a horse. I agree to that. You shall choose the horse.'

'Today is Derby Day.'

'Is it indeed? How very suitable.'

Driving into London from the south, we reached Waterloo and crossed Westminster Bridge. Pa drove through St James's Park and brought the Mini to rest in an empty space in St James's Square. We were delighted to find nearly an hour left on the meter and Pa gave me a tenpenny piece instead of putting it in the slot.

'That's time enough for us,' he said. 'We shan't be long.'

The sun shone; the traffic did not seem to smell quite as terrible as usual as we walked up to Bond Street.

'You must admit,' Pa said, pausing by Scotts, 'that it is tantalising.'

We stood looking at the hats. There was a black, a brown and a grey bowler. A fine, grey top-hat was placed away from the bowlers; the only swan in a gaggle of geese, next to a restrained check-cap and a deerstalker.

'Not really; I expect she is right, she usually is.' Pa took a step forward, hesitated, turned, and went quickly into the shop. I waited on the pavement, sure he would come out muttering some excuse, but he did not. After a few anxious minutes, I went into the shop. Pa stood wearing a Panama and was about to write a cheque.

'Pa!' I protested. 'Really!'

'Just the job isn't it?' Pa turned the brim down all the way round. 'I should be wearing my dog collar.'

'Many of the clergy don't nowadays, sir; just a black polo-neck.'

'That is so.' Pa wrote the cheque and we left the shop with him wearing the hat and holding me firmly by the hand.

'Don't speak,' said Pa, 'my heart is going pit-a-pat; we are nearly there.'

'Not a soul will recognize you. There is no need to be so scared, Pa.'

'But I *am*. I know it is illogical, but this show is far, far worse than your visits to Mr Heath are for you.'

'None of your self-portraits is of you wearing a hat and none is really like you.'

'So you all say, but I don't look like me now, do I, and nor do you look like my lovely pictures of you, but the people, if there are any people, may twig; they just might.'

'No, Pa, they won't. They none of them recognized Ma or Josh. She said you walk round, look at the pictures, and walk out.'

'My knees are knocking together.'

At the gallery the notices said this was the first one-man show of Andrew Fuller's work and a lot of blah about his special talent for depicting family life. I sneered inwardly at that, having heard Pa complain often enough that we were all rotten models. I gave his hand a jerk and we went in.

Pa pulled his sun-glasses out of his pocket and put them on. 'Better be safe than sorry.' He squared his shoulders and we advanced into what I think of now as a magical day.

Apart from a girl with very short hair wearing a lot of make-up (which showed she was not as young as she dressed) sitting at the table selling catalogues, there were only two other people besides ourselves; a short man in jeans and a sweatshirt with 'Bonnie Dundee' stencilled on it, and an immensely tall girl with spectacles, long hair, long skirts and lots of bean necklaces. The man had his arm round the girl's waist, holding his arm high to do so. They swayed round the gallery. 'I like the one of the hipbath.' The girl peered. Pa held my hand and we paused, as though looking at the full-length portrait of Ma in a deck-chair. Pa gave my hand a squeeze.

'Can't say I like that one.' The girl swayed on.

'Somebody did.'

'Sure somebody did. Wish I had that kind of dough. Just look at that! That's alive. That handstand's great. The greatest, isn't it?'

They stood in admiration in front of the picture of me. The framer had framed it upsidedown. Pa had said, 'Let it go, it won't make any odds; nobody will appreciate it in any case.'

'I sure appreciate that one,' said the girl, her bean beads making a gritty noise as they swung across her chest. 'The whole effect is vertigo, sheer genius. Any other painter would have the skirt fall over the kid's face, but not this one! It sure puts a pin in Newton's eye.'

'That's a good expression, the one about the pin. Where did you get it?' Pa was unable to restrain himself.

'Some Western, I guess.' The girl took off her spectacles and looked Pa up and down, smiling. 'Reverend.' Without the glasses her eyes were lovely. She turned away, her skirts trailing, the short man hanging on. She put the glasses back on her nose to peer again at the picture of Ma.

Pa, still holding my hand, moved to the middle of the room and let his eyes rake the walls. His hand began to tremble.

'Is your heart going pit-a-pat?' I was anxious.

'It certainly is. Let's get out of here.' Pa made for the door. I ran after him.

'Got to telephone. Let's go to the Ritz.'

'The Ritz?'

'Lots of telephones. Here, buy a paper.' Pa grabbed an *Evening Standard* from a paper seller.

'You've never been to the Ritz.'

'What's that to us? Lord, Lisa, mind that bus, it nearly got us.' He dragged me through the swing doors, down the hall to the telephones. 'Hold my hat and study the form.'

'Study what?'

'The form, Lisa. Choose a horse, pick the winner. Turn to the racing page. I have to telephone. There's a pin in Newton's eye!' He quoted the girl in the gallery.

I shrugged my shoulders and opened the paper. I had never been in the Ritz and wondered whether the people behind the reception desk knew that we were totally out of place. Then I remembered that we were not looking like us but like a country parson up for the day with his little girl. I turned up the brim of the Panama, put it on and applied myself to the list of horses. In the telphone booth Pa was talking excitedly. I chose a suitable horse: False Start. This horse would win.

Pa came out of the booth. 'Found one?'

'Yes.' I pointed with my finger, noticing without surprise that since leaving home it had grown dirty.

'I can't back a horse called False Start. Let's see the list.' He snatched the paper from me. 'Really, darling, False Start is fifty-to-one. It won't get round the course. Ah, here's one, False Modesty, relation I expect. Oh, it's the favourite. That'll do, have to, we haven't much time. I've got to get the money. We'll have to ring Sandy again.'

'But Pa—'

'What now?' Pa was suddenly furious. I began to cry. 'Oh, all right, it's all some frightful joke anyway, none of it's true. False Start it is. Very apt, I daresay.' He spoke haughtily, grabbing the telephone; talking to Sandy he raised his voice to an angry shout. 'Yes, I know it's mad. In the Ritz. I know it's not my line. No, you wouldn't recognize me. My wife's disguised me as a parson. No, I have not been drinking. Do as I say or I'll fire you.' Pa banged down the receiver.

'Mop up,' he said, handing me his handkerchief. 'We'll buy some lunch and watch the race on your grandfather's television in glorious colour.'

'It's against your principles.'

'So is success, money, all the rotten lot. We should be living in a barn in the country, not in a suburban semi with "Success" on the gate. Hah!'

When he cried 'Hah!' it was time for silence. I was silent.

'Blow the lot,' said Pa. 'Let it blow away as quickly as it

came. It is much healthier, better for the soul.' When Pa spoke of The Soul the storm was over. 'Lunch, and a pin in Newton's eye for a False Start. It will entertain my father, it's his kind of joke.'

'What is?' We were walking along King Street by now, heading for St James's Square.

'He will laugh like a hyena when he hears about my pictures.'

'Hears what, Pa?'

'That I've sold the lot.'

The blood rushed to my face. 'Pa!' I wailed.

'Yes.'

'You sold them?'

'Yes. Didn't you notice all the red blobs in the corners?' Pa stopped outside Spinks and looked down at me. 'Don't worry,' he said kindly. 'It's all on the horse. There may be enough left over to give your Ma a treat, but not to buy her a colour TV.'

'Oh, Pa.' I began to cry bitterly. 'I didn't know. I didn't see. I so hated that girl—'

'Darling, do stop. What a day! First me then you getting strung up. What would you have done if you'd won?'

'Bought a house in the country. Oh, I would, I would.'

'Nothing is as easy as that, love,' said Pa. 'This is real life, with idiotic girls thinking a portrait of my lovely wife is a hipbath and—oh look—we have a parking ticket—' Pa broke into a run, his legs scissoring along like Dr Roger Bannister in an old replay to engage the traffic warden in argumentative protest.

Chapter 2

'I have written the ticket,' said the traffic warden. 'Can't go back on it but I'll make a note of the time: only half an hour. Usually people take three for lunch and then the fine mounts up.'

'But we haven't had lunch,' I said.

'Must be hungry then.'

'Not very. We were backing a horse, that's why we overran our time.' Pa tipped the hat onto the back of his head.

'Which one?' asked the traffic warden.

'False Start.'

'Don't you mean False Modesty? He's the favourite.'

'We know.'

'Got a tip from Above?'

'My daughter chose him.'

'This isn't the pools where you just give the baby a pin.' The warden spoke severely. 'You have to study the form, his breeding and that; do a lot of research.'

'Have you done that?' Pa enquired.

'Of course, in the library here. The London Library, number fourteen,' he prompted.

'Oh.' Pa looked thoughtful.

'Don't think I'm fit to belong to such a posh place, I suppose, holy gent like you. Well I am. That library's a democratic institution, all sorts belong, gents like you, students, lads on bicycles who look like they need a wash—squatters some of them I wouldn't be surprised—chain their bikes to the railings, don't trust nobody and why should they? The world treats them rough.'

'Hold on, hold on,' said Pa meekly. 'I'm in disguise. I'm not a holy gent, I'm a painter.'

'So was Hitler,' said the warden nastily.

'I don't believe I am quite as bad as he was.'

'Ah well, why didn't you say so.' The warden snapped his book shut.

'What's your subject?' asked Pa.

'Toads,' said the warden. 'Very interesting animals. Not many round here, though.'

'When False Start has won we are going to buy a house in the country. Come and stay with us,' I said.

'Okay, I will.'

'What's your address?' Pa asked.

'I'll write it here.' The warden wrote with his finger on the dusty back window of the car: John Bailey, 12 Harrow Buildings, Islington. 'Long way to come to work, but when I go off duty I go into the library; it's handy.'

'Must be.' Pa looked fleetingly envious of the man's good fortune. 'We must go. It's been nice to meet you.' He began to insert himself into the Mini.

'Good luck with your painting,' said the warden, smiling for the first time.

'I've had that,' said Pa. 'It all depends on the horse.'

'Forgive a horse laugh,' called the warden as Pa drove off.

Tears of anger welled up.

'Oh, Lisa, it's not serious.' Pa dodged a large Mercedes. 'If we hurry we can buy some grub and get to your grandfather in time for the parade.'

We stopped in Soho long enough to buy a tin of tunafish, an onion, a carton of cream, and strawberries. We reached the tattered house in Bloomsbury where my grandfather lived on the top floor, defying all efforts of landlords and developers to evict him. 'Only death will get me out,' had been his cry for years, and the vultures, as he called his landlords, waited.

There was no meter free. Pa, careless now, left the Mini under a notice which said 'No Parking', leapt out and pressed the bell.

'He won't be pleased,' I said, clutching the parcels.

'No. Probably won't let us in.'

'Who's that?' Grandpa's aged voice came from a window, high up.

'Me, Grandpa.' I stood out in the street so that he could see me.

'Lisa. What are you doing here?'

'Want to watch the Derby,' I yelled. Then, more tactfully, 'Come to see you.'

'Wait a moment.'

'Oh dear, he takes hours to get downstairs.'

We stood on the steps in the dusty sunshine. The strawberries were getting squashy. Inside the house which, apart from Grandpa's eyrie, was empty, we heard the clatter of shoes as somebody ran downstairs. The door opened.

'Sandy, what are you doing here?' Pa looked surprised.

'Thought you might come here. Thought I might be in time to stop you.'

'Well, you are not.' We trooped inside, the door clanged, echoing up through the empty house. I ran ahead of Pa and Sandy.

'Hullo,' said Grandpa, when I reached his flat. He sat with his back to me, facing the television. I could see the frill of white hair hanging over his collar, the light from the television glinting on his bald head. The curtains were drawn, the room stuffy.

'Just in time,' said Grandpa. 'What have you backed?'

'False Start.'

'Very suitable.'

'The traffic warden who booked us said False Modesty would win.'

'That's the favourite. There's an animal called Embattled I fancy, but you may be right. I also like Iron Duke.'

'Pa said you'd laugh.'

'Why?'

'He's sold all his pictures and put the money on False Start. I didn't know. I chose the horse. I thought it was a joke.' This came out in a rush.

'So that's what that Sandy fellow is fussing about.' Grandpa chuckled. 'Thinks he may lose his commission. No wonder he's sweating.'

I groaned.

'No need to shed tears over him,' Grandpa sniffed. 'He

knows he's on to a good thing with that boy.' By 'that boy' Grandpa meant my father. 'What would you have done if your beast had won,' He spoke as though the race were already in the past.

'Bought a house in the country.'

'Very sensible. You are stranded in Croydon. Not that I don't like the place—learnt to fly there.'

'Learnt to fly?'

'Why not? I haven't always been a poor old man besieged in his home by vultures. If your animal wins I'll come with you. A sniff of fresh air might clear my pipes.'

At this moment Pa and Sandy, who had obviously quarrelled for they looked studiously calm, came into the room.

'Sit down if you can find a chair, but don't talk. I want to watch this.' Grandpa did not turn his head.

'Lisa, are you starving?' Pa took the parcels of food from me.

'I couldn't eat.'

'After the race then.' Pa took the strawberries into Grandpa's kitchen and the room's usual smell of tobacco, garlic and oil reasserted itself. I could hear my father muttering as he searched for a cool place to put the food, 'He really should have a refrigerator, this cream will curdle—'

'Thought you were against electric gadgets,' shouted Grandpa who, like many old people who pretend to be deaf, had the hearing of an animal. 'Turn up the sound you, Sandy Whatsit, and sit quiet.'

Pa joined me on the sofa, feeling with his hand in case he sat on Old X-ray, Grandpa's cat.

'She's here,' I said, 'in my arms.' I laid my cheek for comfort against her stout flank. Old X-ray moved off my lap on to the floor with a plop.

'Do I *have* to go to Mr Heath?'

'You do.' Pa gritted his teeth. Neither of us was having an easy day.

'The traffic warden said you were like Hitler.' Rage

against the injustice of the world beset me. I was glad my pa was going to lose all that money—delighted.

'He meant Hitler was a bad painter. That's what he did before his glorification bit. We might ask him to stay.'

'He's dead isn't he?'

'I meant the warden, stupid.'

'Stay where?'

'In this barrack you are going to buy in the country.'

'So False Start will win?'

'Would be a pin in Newton's eye, wouldn't it?'

Chapter 3

As you will have guessed ever since you read that famous horse's name, False Start won the Derby by five lengths. Embattled came second, Iron Duke third, and False Modesty trailed in last. None of us—except Sandy—actually saw the drama when False Start cast his jockey to the ground, kicked his trainer in the teeth, and bit the lad who was leading him in the arm so badly that it later had to be amputated, before whirling to win. Sandy was the only one who sat through the confusion and noise caused by Old X-ray's ghostly shriek indicating that she was about to give birth to the first, and indeed last, kitten she ever had.

With my grandfather, Pa and myself in attendance, Old X-ray produced one tiny kitten in Grandpa's bed. After licking the kitten dry, she ate a large part of the carton of cream we had bought to eat with our strawberries, then settled, watchful, to rest.

Sandy's garbled description of the race took a little while to penetrate after this extraordinary episode, if such a belittling word can be used for the birth of Old X-ray's progeny, Angelique.

Grandpa, having heard Sandy's story and made sure that all was well with Old X-ray, tiptoed out of the flat and disappeared, while Pa, his head buried in his arms, listened to the television commentators who replayed the race twice. We were too bemused to speak. When Grandpa returned, panting from the long climb up the stairs, carrying a bottle of champagne, Pa revived and was able to mix tuna and chopped onion and fix bowls of strawberries with what was left of the cream.

We felt better after that. Grandpa had backed both Embattled and Iron Duke for a place and won a lot of money which made him very happy. Even Sandy, who had backed False Modesty, was pleased for our family and especially so after an expedition to the nearest telephone to ring up his bookmaker. Pa, by backing False Start with the entire proceeds of the sale had made, as Sandy put it, 'a bomb, oh BOY!' For the sake of Old X-ray who, Grandpa said, would need quiet, we ate and drank almost in silence until, laying down his spoon, Sandy ventured to say, 'Why do you not have the telephone, sir?'

'I do not have the telephone'—Grandpa raised his voice to a harsh shout, forgetting Old X-ray and her kitten—'because fools like you might ring me up, my landlords might make threatening calls, my friends might invite me to their deathbeds—we have all reached that age—I might be tempted to invite people here; I would lose the use of my legs—'

'Your legs?'

'Staggering up and down that appalling flight of stairs is the only exercise I get. Young people are fools.'

'Sorry, sir, I truly am.' Sandy was stupefied by this outburst.

'Now you have assured yourself that my son is able to pay you, perhaps you will leave. Nobody invited you here. Take yourself off. Go elsewhere. Find some other door to put your foot in.' There was silence as Sandy left. We heard his feet tapping down the stairs and the street door close.

'Do I *have* to go to the dentist?' I asked in the vacuum which followed Grandpa's rudeness.

'Yes, you do,' cried Pa, catching Grandpa's rage like a virus infection. 'You do indeed, you spoilt brat, eating strawberries and cream like a pig, betting,'—he made it sound like a mortal sin—'watching television. Hah!' He sprang to his feet, seized the television, lurched to the window and cast it out.

We watched, holding our breath, as the television, missing our Mini by an inch, smashed into smithereens in the street.

'Sorry, Father.' Pa spoke very mildly.

Grandpa grinned. 'Worth it, dear boy. I like a man of principle. Besides, you can afford to buy me another.' He stooped to kiss my forehead. 'Off you go to the dentist. I shall come and stay with you. Why are you wearing those clothes, dear boy? You look like a cleric. I rather like the hat though. Will you give it to me?'

'No,' said Pa. 'This hat is mine; it's a lucky hat.'

A thought struck me as we trotted down the stairs.

'Pa, it must be a lucky hat. I was wearing it when I chose False Start.'

'You were?'

'Yes.'

'Magic?'

I nodded.

Chapter 4

Driving to Hampstead, where Mr Heath lurked, I saw, reflected in the driving mirror, the tracings of the traffic warden's finger. 'Shall we invite John Bailey to stay?'

'The fellow who said I was like Hitler? Why not? He will get on well with my father and, if he likes toads, with you and Josh.'

'May I choose the house? There are lots in the *Country Lifes* in the waiting room.'

'It makes me ill to look at all those stately lots.'

'Some of them are quite small.'

'You know I can't even afford to look.'

'You can now you are rich.'

'So I am.' Pa let go of the wheel and patted the Panama with both hands. A car driving beside us swerved and the driver let down his window to shout, 'Made your will?'

Pa pretened not to notice. 'Where do you want to live?' he asked.

'As far from Mr Heath as possible.' The heights of Hampstead were growing near.

'Ungrateful child,' said Pa, quoting my school dentist. 'One of the few juveniles to have the Heath process from milk teeth to molars.'

'Ugh!'

'It would be sad if his trouble was wasted and my trouble too, bringing you here every three months.'

The dreaded Mr Heath, I shall have to explain, as I have not had time to before, was carrying out an experiment on children's teeth, painting them with his own anti-rot invention from the moment they pushed through infant gums to the time they reached adulthood. The process was painless, but before painting on his 'brew' as he called it, Mr Heath would explore our mouths with sharp instruments and podgy fingers. The brew was bright red and after each application we looked as though we had chewed betel nut.

The parents of his volunteers, as we were called, were able to claim a small travel allowance, and Mr Heath averred that this enabled many children to go to the pantomime who would otherwise have missed it. This laughable theory made us wonder whether the experiment was not a fraud of some sinister kind.

'We could also have Mr Heath to stay.' Pa parked the Mini. 'And kill him off.'

The waiting room was full of leather-covered chairs and tidy piles of *Country Life*, *Vogue* and *Private Eye*, to show, Josh said, Mr Heath's sophistication. I sank gloomily into a chair while Pa gave my name to the receptionist who knew it perfectly well but pretended to have forgotten.

'And how is Mrs Fuller?' she asked.

'She was all right when we left home,' said Pa.

'Oh good.' The receptionist's voice was high.

'She won't be when we get back.' The receptionist, not sure whether this was a joke, gave a half smile. 'Mr Heath won't keep you long.' She always said this. We always arrived early and there was always time for *Country Life*.

'Lend me the hat,' I whispered. Humouring a fractious child, Pa handed me the Panama. Though it reached my nose in front and the nape of my neck behind, I could, as I had found when looking at the *Evening Standard* in the Ritz, balance it on my ears.

I concentrated on *Country Life*, turning the pages slowly. A Georgian manor in Hampshire, a grange in the Cotswolds, a Tudor manor in Kent, an abbey on the Welsh border, desirable residences all over the British Isles. I sighed, turning up the brim of the hat. Perhaps no residence desired us, the Fuller family.

In the corner of the last page was a blurred photograph of a house, one end of which looked kind, the other, partly hidden by a tree, cross. As I peered at it from under the brim of the hat I thought someone called my name, 'Lisa, Lisa', from a long way off, 'Lisa'. The call seemed to come from the house in the photograph. I suppressed the idea as idiotic. All the same, 'This is it,' I said to Pa, handing him the magazine.

'Haphazard House?' Pa queried, holding the photograph up. 'Darling, too grim for words—we'd hate it.'

'Put the hat on.' I handed him the Panama.

'Dearest, it will be sold. This is a year old.' He waved the magazine.

'Put it on,' I said. Pa perched the hat on his head and looked again.

'I see what you mean.' Pa smiled. The receptionist called. I went meekly to my doom.

Mr Heath had a new chair. One sat, swung up one's legs and lay back. I felt helpless.

'Ah, Lisa Fuller, aged ten.' The plump voice throbbed from a throat buried in a thick neck.

'Eleven,' I said.

'Ah yes, eleven of course. Age is so important when one is growing up. Open wide. Let's have a look at your gnashers.' He sounded eager. I opened up. 'No trouble of course.' This was a statement. 'What a happy little girl you must be.'

I closed my mouth.

'Open o-o-pen wide. Your lovers will bless me for my care.'

Rage and affront gripped me. His impertinence pried my feelings as his pick explored my teeth. 'I have no lovers.' I clenched my jaws.

'But you will have. That's what it's all about, you must know that, dear.' Fruity reproof.

'I am not *dear.*' My face was red, tears close.

'Oh, sorry. I must remember that. The acids released by bad temper affect the teeth. I have told you that before.'

'No, you haven't.'

'Come on, Lisa, I haven't got all night.' He sounded almost human. I unclenched my jaws. My mouth was full of spit.

'Rinse,' Mr Heath said patiently. He had a new rinse instead of the pink I was used to. This was orange.

'Nice, isn't it?' He noticed my surprise. 'Come on, Lisa.' I submitted. The sharp steel pick tiptapped round my teeth, pausing, probing. With his left hand reaching round my neck from behind, he held a mirror pressing roughly down on my lower lip. He was getting his revenge; he always did.

'You will be grateful to old Heath one day.' He always said this.

I closed my eyes. He was using a new kind of soap, more expensive than the one I was used to. He released me.

'Do you have private patients? What do you charge them?'

'Pry, pry, pry. None of your business. Open wide.'

'It's immoral.'

'Been reading the papers, eh? Open, please.'

'I'm a guinea pig. I'm entitled to know.'

'Come on, Lisa. I want to paint on my brew; it's a new colour.'

'What?'

Mr Heath deftly wedged my jaws open with a wodge of gauze. 'Now keep still,' he said grimly. 'Your brother behaves much better than you.' The painting began.

Suddenly anxious to get the whole stupid business over, I lay back. Mr Heath was silent, earnest and concentrated. At last he said, 'There. That wasn't so awful was it? See you in three months. Oh, just a teeny fraction left out; you distracted me by your naughty talk.' He pulled the light down on its stalk.

I caught sight of a weird reflection in the burnished steel of the light shade—Mr Heath's nose bending over me, his podgy fingers painting the last teeny bit of tooth—blue.

I snapped my teeth, tasting the expensive soap, and blood. He shrieked. Pa gave a roar of laughter when he and the receptionist dashed in in answer to the shriek. After delightedly watching the application of elastoplast, we got a frigid farewell.

'Well,' said Pa, slamming the Mini door which was apt to stick. 'That is the end of that panto. Let us make the day complete with a visit to Squire, Close and Sword.'

'Who are they?' My feeling of triumph was short-lived and regret was creeping on.

'Is your soul troubled with remorse?'

'A bit.'

'Don't give it another thought; the man's a charlatan. On, on to the faithful Squire etc. They, too, like the famous library, are within reach of St James'. Perhaps we shall meet the warden again. We could tell him we won.'

'Who are—?'

'The house agents of course. Through them we buy the house, Haphazard.'

Chapter 5

Squire, Close and Sword were shut when we reached them at five-past-five. We had left the Mini in St James's Square and as we walked back to it we saw the traffic warden sticking something under the wiper. He waited for us. Pa took the paper—a short note. 'Did you win much?'

'A tremendous lot,' I said.

'Thought that somehow. What will you do with it, if it's not rude to ask?'

'Buy a house in the country, but the agents are shut. We are going to ask you to stay.' I smiled at Mr Bailey. He rocked back on his heels.

'Whatever have you done to your teeth?'

We explained. We told him about the race, the kitten, the dentist and how I had bitten Mr Heath. The traffic warden laughed a lot and agreed that I was not cut out to be a guinea-pig.

'What about this house, then?' he asked.

'We shall have to come back tomorrow—if my wife agrees.'

'If I was you I wouldn't tell her,' said the warden. 'Present her with a *fait accompli*. I study French, too.'

'Ma speaks French. You can talk to each other when you come.'

'I should like that, but would she?'

We assured him that she would and, promising to meet next day, set off home.

We arrived late for tea and too early for supper. My mother gave an exclamation of pain when she saw my teeth. 'What on earth has he done this time?'

'She bit the man. That is the stain of his blue blood.'

'Ma, we—'

'And *where* did you get that hat, Andrew? You look quite weird.'

'Bought it to wear at the show.' Pa took it off and handed it to Ma.

'Really, darling.' She handled the hat with curious fingers. 'It's a real Panama; a fearful waste of money.'

'Put it on,' I said, taking it from her and placing it on her head. She made as if to refuse, but a funny look came over her face and the expression of tired exasperation left her. She seemed far away. She put her hands up and felt the hat, her eyes astonished.

'What's the matter?' Josh who, at fourteen, was as tall as Ma, took the hat and put it on.

'It's,' she began. 'I was—I thought—no, I *saw*. It was a bit vague, but—'

We heard Josh give a grunt of surprise and watched his face as he, too, wearing the hat, put his hands up to it.

'What a super house.' Josh's voice was joyous. 'Where is it?'

Pa was as surprised as I by Ma, Josh and the hat, for when Pa and I had worn it we had seen nothing, only felt.

'Try it on Bogus,' I suggested. Bogus was a sad, uneasy dog who had never forgotten that he was a lost dog until Josh visited Battersea Dogs' Home one winter afternoon. We lavished love, walks, treats of all kinds on him, but Bogus had always been a faraway dog, looking upon us kindly but not with devotion. He made us feel we would do until his lost master turned up, but no more. He was standing a little apart from us, his tail neither up nor down, his eyes tolerant.

Ma knelt down. 'Come here, Bogus, look at this.' She took the hat from Josh and gave it to Bogus to sniff. He backed away. She held it a little above him and he cringed as though she were going to hit him. Then, suddenly, as she stood holding the hat, Bogus went wild. He gave a yelp which turned into full throttle barks. He threshed his tail, he jumped up and down, greeting each one of us in turn as though he had waited long years for us. He ran in circles; he lovingly licked our hands and faces; he grew visibly younger and tremendously jolly. The sad, thoughtful, lost dog from Battersea had gone.

The scene with Bogus lasted quite a long time and we moved into the kitchen, a poky room looking on to a strip of garden where nothing grew.

Ma put the hat down and, taking Pa's hand, said, 'And now begin.' Still whimpering in his throat, Bogus pressed his chin on Pa's knee. The tale came out disjointedly. Pa told and I told. We told about the traffic warden and the pictures. Josh interrupted.

'But the *hat*? And where—is—that—house I saw?'

'It is Haphazard House,' I cried. 'Did it look kind on one side and not on the other?'

'Well the other side is hidden by a tree—'

'We are going to buy it,' I said.

'Money?' Ma was ironical.

'False Start won at fifty-to-one, didn't he?'

'You bet? Where did you get the money?'

The whole story came out, the sale of the pictures, the money put on False Start, the parking ticket, Old X-ray's kitten, *Country Life*, my biting Mr Heath and the tragic moment when we found Squire, Close and Sword shut. 'Mind you, I don't believe any of it really happened,' Pa ended rather sadly.

'Yes, it did. Look at Bogus. You bought a magic hat and solved our problems. We move to Haphazard House and live happily ever after,' said Ma.

'That magazine was over a year old. The house will be sold.'

Ma snatched up the hat and put it on Pa's head. He smiled and said, 'You are right of course.'

'Oh, I'm so hungry.' Josh let out a cry. 'Starving.' We had been sitting talking until supper-time was long past.

'I wish tomorrow would come,' I said as I helped get supper. 'I won't feel safe until Haphazard is ours.'

'If it has been bought by someone else we will buy it back.'

'You talk as though you know all about it. *I* found it,' I said.

'But *I've* seen it,' said Josh.

'What about Bogus,' said Ma peaceably. 'If that dog could talk I believe he could tell us all about it.' As we sat down to supper Bogus reached up and took the hat off the table to his basket where he lay with it, his nose resting blandly on its crown.

Chapter 6

'Darling,' said my mother to Pa, 'be an angel and take off that suit before you eat. You might spill something down your front.' She held a china ladle she had found in a junk shop over the saucepan of soup.

'Does it matter?'

'Well—yes.'

'You said you bought it for forty pence at a jumble sale.'

'A white lie. Do please take it off.'

'Then where did you get it?'

Josh and I listened, grinning, to this exchange. Pa's clothes were always jeans and jersey in winter and jeans and tee-shirt in summer. To avoid recognition at his show Ma had produced the suit from, she said, a jumble sale. 'The soup will get cold if you don't buck up.' Ma was brisk.

'You insist I change my clothes before supper?' He was belligerent.

'Well, yes.' She was firm.

'Why?' Pa's voice rose.

'Because,' said Ma, putting the ladle back in the saucepan and returning the saucepan to the stove as though preparing for a long argument, 'because I hired it from Moss Bros.'

'You did *what*?'

'Where else would I get a suit for a man of your height?'

'My principles—' Pa gasped. 'You'd think I had gone to a levee, to the Royal Academy. Hah!'

There was a long pause while they glared at each other.

Then Ma said mildly, 'Well, love, you bought a hat to go with it. You were glad enough of the disguise when I provided it, so take it off now and we can get on with supper. You seem to have forgotten your principles when you wanted to watch the Derby on your father's TV.'

'Suppose I say that giving my principles a rest is good for my soul?'

'I'd still say look sharp and change because we are all hungry and want to celebrate your success. I bought a consolation bottle. Now we will celebrate with it.'

'All right, you win.' Pa stood up. 'And that reminds me—I have to buy a television.'

'A television?' Our mother looked astonished.

'What's happened to him?' asked Josh, but Pa had left the room.

'Is it for us?' Josh asked me. I shook my head, thinking it more tactful that Pa should explain his action at Grandfather's himself. He was capable of a version of his own. He, too, might tell a white lie; find it expedient to say the television had fallen out of the window by itself. If his painting of Ma could be mistaken for a hipbath, he might see his action of the afternoon differently from me.

'What's a hipbath?' I asked.

'Before H & C, stupid,' said Josh, 'people sat in hipbaths in front of a roaring fire and washed in parts.'

'Oh,' I said, none the wiser.

'Why did you want to know?' Our mother stood by the stove, gently stirring the soup.

'There was a tall girl at the show who thought the portrait of you was a hipbath. She was pretending to be American. She was with a short man. They were the only people there.'

'Oh.' Ma stirred. 'It would be nice to know who bought the pictures. Did your father ask?'

'No.'

'Soup.' Pa came back wearing jeans and a jersey, his hair ruffled. 'Soup.' He carried the pepper-and-salt suit reverently like a fireman carrying an unconscious child from a blaze. 'Where shall I put it?'

'Put it on the hall table. We can return it tomorrow.'

'I forgive you. That was a very wicked thing to do, tripping me by my principles.' Pa was happy now in his old clothes.

Bogus in his basket gave a satisfied groan and settled himself more comfortably. 'I would love to know—' Josh looked at Bogus, 'where he came from.'

'A hat shop, obviously.' Ma ladled out onion soup and passed round toast and grated cheese.

'It might be something about the hat,' I agreed.

Bogus, like many lost dogs, was of unknown breed. When Josh visited the Dogs' Home he came away with Bogus. Why not some other dog? Why this particular one, we had asked. How could he bear to go to such a place?

Josh had looked at the dogs, poodles and terriers and mongrels galore. They had all been very eager to come. They asked by whining and yelping and wagging their tails, standing against the bars. They had begged to become gladly, obligingly, Josh's dog. Josh, who was thirteen at the time, had found the choice impossible. He knew that he could only have one dog, one which was not too large and expensive to feed. A dog who was, if possible, young. Josh had had no idea what all those dogs wanting him for a master would do to him; the pressure of having to make a choice was great. He burst into tears and turned to leave, to get away from that hopeful barking, those wagging tails.

But then he saw Bogus. Bogus had not barked, yelped or wagged his tail. 'He was sitting there,' Josh told us, 'just sitting there looking at me, and then he turned away, as though I wouldn't do.'

Josh wiped his tears, paid the money and got the man in charge to ring up Ma to confirm that the dog would have a responsible family. He led Bogus home to Croydon and not once did Bogus look pleased or grateful. We made him welcome and he tolerated us. His coat was long and silky like a collie and his tail abnormally long. His ears could never make up their mind whether to stand up like an Alsatian's or to flop across the top of his head like the flaps of a deerstalker. His paws had been worn when he was brought in, the Dogs' Home man said, the nails raw. He had only one claim to beauty—his eyes. Bright, intelligent eyes which, undoglike, outstared us from under a fine fringe. When, that evening, we settled down to supper, and Bogus in his basket groaned, we realized that if by selling all the pictures and putting the money on False Start our lives had changed, Bogus's life had changed, too.

'Tomorrow,' said Pa, holding out his bowl for more soup, 'tomorrow we shall all go to Messrs Squire, Close and Sword to buy Haphazard House and take Bogus with us.'

'Hear, hear,' said Josh, and Bogus, hearing his name mentioned, groaned again.

'Did you say—' our mother gave our father more soup, 'did you say you had to buy a television? Not like you, is it?'

'I threw my father's out of the window.' Pa accepted the soup.

'You know, love, your manic exaggerations are a fearfully bad example to the children. More soup, Lisa?'

'Yes, please,' I said and passed my plate.

Chapter 7

We set off, squashed into the Mini, parents in front, Ma driving, Josh, Bogus and me behind. Pa wore the hat.

Ma drove into London, via Chelsea, Eaton Square, down the Mall and up into St James's Square; not as Pa had driven the day before, over by Westminster Bridge, his favourite. Driving round the square, we passed the warden sticking a ticket under the wiper of a Rolls. Ma found a space.

'Morning,' shouted Pa.

The warden looked up and scowled. 'That meter's out of order,' he said.

'Oh, good,' I said.

'Oh, it's you,' said the warden, relaxing the folds round his nose in a smile. 'Didn't recognize you in that get-up. Going slumming or something?' He looked at our parents.

'No, no, this is the real me,' said Pa. 'What you saw yesterday was a disguise. May I introduce my wife? Darling, this is Mr Bailey who we told you about.' Ma held out her hand. 'And my son Josh, and our dog Bogus.'

The warden shook our hands and stooped to pat Bogus who endured it. 'Going to buy your house then?'

'Yes,' we nodded.

'Come and stay, Mr Bailey. I hear you are interested in toads,' said Ma.

'I am. Toads and grass snakes. I'm a bit of an ornithologist, too, but you don't get much opportunity in London: sparrows, thrushes, blackbirds, mostly.'

'Will the car be all right here?' asked Pa.

'I'll keep an eye on it. Can't give you a ticket if the meter don't tick over, can I? This one,' he smacked the Rolls, 'been here hours. Some people are made of money. I forgot, you're rich yourself.' He grinned at Pa and moved away.

'That job represents power,' said Pa. 'Come on.'

We trooped in single file to Squire, Close and Sword, just off the square. The office had thick pile carpet. A young man sat at a desk with three telephones on it, and a girl sat at another, typing—tip-tap-tippity-tap.

'Can I help you?' The young man rose, his eyes—taking in our group—took us for people who had come in to ask the way. He looked with distaste at Bogus, and aloofly at Pa in his jeans. He clearly thought our mother pretty, Josh and I not worthy of attention.

'I want to buy a house called Haphazard House.' Pa spoke from a foot above the young man's head.

'Haphazard House?' The young man—little more than a youth—shook his head. 'I don't think—'he began.

'Ask someone who knows.'

'Oh yes. Will you wait a moment? Take a seat.' He indicated an armchair near the door. We remained standing. 'I'll ask.' He picked up one of the telephones. 'Mr Spruce? There's—er—a person here asking about a house—Haphazard House. Is it on our books, sir? Shall I? Oh—yes sir, certainly, at once.' He looked dismayed. 'Will you come this way, please?' We followed him.

'What name, please?' he asked dubiously.

'Fuller. Andrew Fuller.'

We reached a door with 'B. Spruce' written on it. The youth knocked, a voice said, 'Come in'. The youth said, 'Mr Andrew Fuller, sir,' and stood aside to let us pass.

A very suave man stood up behind a grand desk and, catching sight of Pa, sprang forward, exclaiming, 'Fuller, Not *the* Andrew Fuller?'

'Well,' said Pa, 'I'm not Fullers' Cakes. I just paint.'

'That's what I mean. I am thrilled to meet you! I was at your exhibition only two days ago. Alas, for me—of course not for you—every picture was sold. I had hoped, well hoped—' His voice trailed as his eyes took in our group. 'What an extraordinary dog! Oh, I beg your pardon, and is this Mrs Fuller?' He shook hands with Ma.

'We are the little Fullers,' Josh introduced us.

'Won't you all sit down?' Mr Spruce ranged chairs in a semicircle.

'Thanks.' We all sat down. Bogus remained standing, staring at Mr Spruce from under his eyebrows.

'Haphazard House,' said Pa. 'I want to buy it.'

'You advertised it in *Country Life*,' I said.

'In what issue?'

'An old one.' Pa was patient.

'Oh, I see.' Mr Spruce smiled. He obviously saw nothing except us, and we were not the kind of people he was used to. He pressed a button. 'Elizabeth, look up Haphazard House—yes, that's what I said.' His voice grew acid. 'These girls—' he said to Ma. 'One cannot get a good secretary these days. The turnover in a firm like this is so big the name had slipped my mind.'

'Is it sold?' asked Josh. Mr Spruce, who obviously had no wish to do business with children, gave an irritated frown. 'If it was advertised in an old issue—'

'At the dentist,' I said.

'There you are. They hang on to their old mags until they fall to pieces. People don't mind what they look at when they are waiting for the chair.' Pa looked stony.

'I read *Private Eye*,' said Josh. 'The dentist's called Heath.' Mr Spruce ignored him.

A girl with red hair walked into the room. 'This what you want?' She plonked a pile of papers in front of Mr Spruce and walked out. 'You see what I mean?' Mr Spruce looked at Ma.

'Like to paint her,' said Pa. 'You don't see many of those Burne Jones types.'

'But she can't even spell.' Mr Spruce looked again towards Ma for sympathy.

'Nor can I,' said Ma, giving none.

'Well,' Mr Spruce pulled himself together. 'Let's see now. Haphazard House. Great hall, one half demolished in 1949, kitchen, eight bedrooms, barns, walled garden—'

'Where is it?' I asked.

'On the Devon and Cornwall borders. Rather remote, I fear. Ah yes, let's see. Twenty acres, mostly woodland. Would make unusual gentleman's residence.' His eyebrows rose. 'That might have been better put.'

'I'm an unusual gentleman,' said Pa. 'Is it still for sale?'

'Well, yes it is. I must in all honesty tell you this house needs a lot doing to it. It has no electricity.'

'Suits me.'

'No main drainage.'

'Don't mind that.'

'It's own water supply.'

'Fine. No filthy chloride.'

'No road to it, just a track.'

'We don't mind that,' Josh and I chorused.

'The house was struck by lightning in 1949 and partly burned down. Nothing has been done to it since.'

'Why not?' I was curious.

'Well, the owner died and, I remember now, the cousin who inherited it put it in our hands to sell.'

'Fine, fine,' Pa fidgeted. 'I'll buy it.'

'We will have it,' I said. 'We said so.'

'Yes, you did.' Mr Spruce didn't seem to like children, but that was okay by me.

'The house,'—Mr Spruce addressed himself to my parents—'is furnished.'

'What with?'

'Well, beds, tables, chairs. You have to take the furniture with the house.'

'I expect it's worm-eaten,' said Josh.

'We can sell it if we don't like it,' I said. Mr Spruce looked pained and sucked in his breath.

'If it had been valuable the cousin would have flogged it,' said Josh.

'Of course he would,' I agreed. 'It's probably very ugly.' I looked round Mr Spruce's office. I didn't think much of his taste—characterless and respectable. I wondered how he could have liked my father's pictures.

'Where did he come from, this heir?' asked Josh.

'Los Angeles, I believe.' Mr Spruce looked at Pa, not caring for Josh any more than me.

'Have you seen it?' I asked.

'No.' He looked at Ma like a witness in court answering to the Judge when questioned by Counsel.

'We'll have it,' said Pa.

'I'll give you an order to view, of course.'

'We'll have it, I said.' Pa was growing irritable.

'I must tell you, Mr Fuller, we must be strictly honest that the house is supposed to be haunted.'

'Hah! I said I'd buy it. Why beat about the bush? You

want to sell it, don't you? How much? I'll give you a cheque and have done with it.'

'It's not as easy as that. You have to have the documents drawn up—'

'Look,' said Pa ominously. 'I have the money, right? You get on with the legal side. You settle with my wife. She may not be able to spell but she's not stupid. Just tell me how much.' He produced his cheque book with the panache of a villain drawing his gun.

Mr Spruce mentioned a huge sum. Pa wrote a cheque, handed it to Mr Spruce, rose to his feet and said, 'Thanks, Spruce. You settle with my wife. All right, darling?' Ma nodded. 'Then we'll meet you at my father's flat. I want to see Old X-ray. Giving birth at her age isn't easy, when it's for the first time.'

We trooped out. 'She'll soon settle his hash,' said Pa. 'Come on, we'll take the car. She can take a taxi.'

'A ghost, how super!' Josh jogged towards the Mini with Bogus.

'Just a selling point. When a property won't move they throw in a ghost to give it something it hasn't got.'

'Haphazard hasn't got a lot of things.' Josh waited while Bogus sniffed at a lamp-post.

'Haphazard will be all right when it's got us.' Pa began to sing. 'I had plenty of money, I poured it down the drain—' He leapt into the air and did an *entrechat*. 'I don't believe that fellow liked us, Lisa. I don't think he took to Bogus or your teeth, your true-blue Tory teeth.' He caught my hand in one of his and Josh's in the other and we danced in a circle round Bogus's lamp-post. Bogus stopped what he was about to do and began to bay.

'Come on, for goodness sake, we will attract a crowd.' Pa ran to the Mini as though pursued.

'Did you get it?' asked the warden, who was prowling by.

'Yes,' said Josh. 'It's got a ghost.'

'That's nice.' The warden didn't believe him. 'And toads?'

'Forgot to ask. Sorry,' said Pa.

'Sure to be toads.' Josh began pushing Bogus into the Mini.

'Dog will like it there.' The warden looked wistful.

'This is the address.' Pa snatched a parking ticket from a nearby windscreen and wrote, Haphazard House, Coldharbour, Devon/Cornwall border.

'Coldharbour? You being funny?'

'No, that's on the prospectus. It's half-burned down, a ruin more or less.'

'Toads like ruins.' The warden memorized the address and put the ticket back under the windscreen.

'So do birds,' said Josh, getting in beside Bogus, 'and snakes.'

'Will you tell my wife when she comes to take a taxi?'

'Okay,' said the warden. 'You left her any money to pay for it?'

Pa clapped his hand to his head. 'No, I haven't. Oh Lord!'

'I'll advance it,' said the warden, already a family friend.

'That's very good of you.'

'You repay me when I come and stay. I'll ring up from Coldharbour.'

'I don't know whether there's a telephone. There's no electricity, no drains and no road.' Pa pressed the starter and the Mini leapt to life.

'You sure there's a house?' The warden was sarcastic.

'Quite sure.' Pa settled the hat firmly on his head and shot backwards into the traffic.

Chapter 8

When we reached Grandpa's house Josh rang the bell while Pa eased the Mini into a gap beside a van painted with nymphs and daisies. This odd conveyance housed the neighbourhood cats when it rained and served as a place to chat on summer evenings for a squatting community befriended by our grandfather. Though refusing to leave his flat, he felt an affinity towards the squatters since they, too, were threatened with eviction.

While we waited on the doorstep the owner of the nymph-and-daisy van came up carrying a plastic bag.

'You going up to old Mr Fuller?'

'Yes, if he'll let us in.'

'His cat's ill.'

'Old X-ray?'

'Yes. This is for her. Will you take it up. I'm late for a date.'

'What is it?'

'Chicken livers to tempt her appetite. She's refusing food.'

'All right,' I said. The young man ran off. 'Pa, Old X-ray's ill.'

'Doesn't he answer the bell?' Our parent was impatient. 'I'm not surprised she's ill, having a kitten at her age.' Pa stepped back into the street, cupped his hands and roared, 'FATHER!'

A window opened and a bunch of keys shot down to clink in the street. Pa opened the front door and we raced up.

Grandpa sat hunched in his armchair with Old X-ray in his arms. His face was all lines and furrows, tears coursed down beside his nose to drop on his chest. His veined and bony hands held Old X-ray stretched across his knees, her eyes shut, body limp. She looked like a sad, little body swept to the side of the street after failing to make the necessary dash to safety. Grandpa did not look up. In one hand he held the kitten close to Old X-ray's flank. It made futile swimming movements with its paws. Its eyes were still shut.

'We brought the chicken livers.' Josh held out the bag.

'Too late I think.' Grandpa was gruff.

Pa took off the hat and knelt beside Grandpa to look closer. Old X-ray's breathing was so frail we could hardly see it.

'She used to romp in that van,' Grandpa muttered. 'She

seemed to enjoy herself. Not much of a life for a cat of spirit, living alone with an old man. She was bored so I let her romp.'

'Father.' Pa gently removed Old X-ray from Grandpa, holding her, kitten and all, close to his chest.

'Is she dead?' Grandpa's eyes were so full of tears he could not see. I heard Josh gulp. He smacked the bag of livers angrily down on the floor. Bogus stood up on his hind legs against Pa. He took Old X-ray from Pa and carrying her—tail and legs limp, head nodding in death—put her into Pa's hat on the floor. Then he came back and removed the kitten and put it, too, into the hat, nosed it against Old X-ray and stood back, his tail wagging, staring hopefully. Nothing happened. Bogus barked loudly in Old X-ray's ear. Old X-ray opened her eyes, sneezed, shot out a paw and scratched Bogus, turned to the kitten and licked its head roughly. The kitten began to suck, and Old X-ray to purr. We let out our breath.

Old X-ray looked at us with contempt, curled herself comfortably in the hat and finishing with the kitten, lifted a back leg and began to wash.

'One would almost think,' Grandpa blew his nose hugely, 'that hat had some special quality.'

'I bought it at a perfectly respectable shop,' said Pa defensively. 'I didn't want people to recognize me at my exhibition. A hat seemed better than a false nose. I'm a shy man.'

'What do you want a false nose for?' In his relief, Grandpa was more than ready to pick a quarrel.

'I didn't want a false nose.' Pa rose to the bait.

'Now, now.' Ma came into the room. 'What's going on? There's a girl downstairs who says Old X-ray is ill.'

'Well, she isn't.' Grandpa was belligerent. 'How on earth can you live with a man with a false nose? You should have more sense. I told you what he was like when you agreed to marry him.'

'You've been crying.' Ma attacked in her turn.

'Hay fever,' said Grandpa.

'The girl said something about chicken livers. Has Old X-ray had any?' Ma had made her point.

'Not yet.' Grandpa looked contrite.

'Shall I chop some?'

'Yes, please.'

Ma took the livers and went into the kitchen. I followed.

'What's all this in aid of?' said Ma.

I told her.

'Well,' she said, slicing livers. 'Well, why not?' She expected no answer and we took the liver to Old X-ray who ate it noisily. Since Bogus was drooling, he got some, too.

'Have you heard,' said Ma, after giving Grandpa a searching look to assure herself he was all right, 'have you heard that we are on the move to the country?'

'That fellow,' said Grandpa, after listening to the story of our buying Haphazard House, 'that fellow who bought these livers—saved the cat's life.' Ma quelled us with a look. 'That young fellow does moving jobs, owns the van outside, the one painted with daisies and birds. He could move your furniture. He and two people I know at the "squat" can help,' said Grandpa, revived.

'It doesn't move,' exclaimed Josh. 'It just sits there.'

'That's what you think.' Grandpa laughed like a concertina with a tear in it. 'Doesn't move! They put spare tyres on and whoops, off they go!'

'Who are they?'

'Tall girl who pretends to be American. And a short chap, and that young David. You could put the odds and bobs like your easel in that.'

'Thanks.' Pa was huffy.

'I bet it's the man and the girl we saw at the exhibition,' I said. 'She called Pa "Reverend", Grandpa, she—'

'What would she have called him if he'd worn his false nose? Coco?'

'Don't start that again.' Ma was firm. 'You'll wake Old X-ray.'

'Got room for me in this chateau of yours?' said Grandpa, unrepentent. 'I'm coming, too. Seems to me none of us can do without this Panama so we'd better stick together,' which was as near to admitting the magic of the hat as he was prepared to go.

'We'd love it,' I said.

'Right. I'll travel in the van with my cats.'

'I wonder what the village of Coldharbour will say when they see us arriving,' Josh pondered.

'Don't make difficulties, boy. They will think we are strolling players, especially if your father wears his false nose. Or a pop group.'

Ma put her arms round Grandpa and kissed him. 'Just stop, darling,' she whispered. 'We've all had rather an exhausting day. I'll make some tea and we can watch your lovely television.'

'You can't. That clown threw it out of the window.'

Chapter 9

When it was time for us to go home to Croydon, Ma gently lifted Old X-ray out of the hat and put her on Grandpa's sofa. Old X-ray's sides began to heave and she gave a pitiful mew.

'She was happy in the hat; what do you want to disturb her for?'

Pa put Old X-ray back in the Panama where she instantly revived.

We looked at one another. Nobody spoke for a while. Grandpa gazed into some faraway land. Pa, with his hands behind his head, stretched his long legs, arched his back, and finally said, 'Ahem.'

Josh and I clattered downstairs with Bogus. When Pa or Ma said 'ahem' it meant they would rather discuss something without us being there. Propping open the front door with an empty milk bottle, we sat on the steps to watch the world go by, with Bogus between us on his hunkers. People passed carrying parcels, lurching on aged legs. Neither Josh nor I was prepared to speak first.

Presently we heard voices and, from the basement occupied by squatters, two figures emerged. I recognized the tall girl and the short man who had been at the exhibition.

'That's the girl and the man who thought Pa's portrait of Ma was a bathtub,' I said.

'Thought you said hipbath. It's not the same thing.'

The man reached up and put his arm round the girl's waist. She laughed. 'Edward, don't do that.'

'Makes me feel dependent,' said the man. The girl laughed again. They walked across the street to the van.

'Time it had a wash,' said the man who, though short, looked strong, with thick arms and legs and a bushy beard.

'It looks okay. It would be different if we were going to use it. Picturesque is what it is.'

Unable to restrain himself, Josh got up and went across to them. Bogus and I followed. 'Our grandfather says you might help us to move,' he said abruptly.

The two looked startled. 'Is that old man the Council are evicting your grandfather?'

'Yes.'

'Oh dear.' The girl looked sympathetic. 'He's lost the battle. Got to move. Like us in the squat. It's final. Any day now we all go. But where, one asks? Where?'

'He hasn't told us.'

'He's valiant. He wouldn't want to upset you. He has to go to alternative accommodation. He'll hate it. We all like him. He invites us up to watch his television and see his cat. Some vandal threw his telly out of the window. Can you believe it?' The girl swayed in her long skirt. She no longer talked American. 'It smashed to bits. Might have hit the van.' Edward patted it, his hand leaving marks on its dusty bonnet.

'Don't you ever get a parking ticket?' Josh wished to change the subject.

'The character who shares the van, David,'—Edward waved his arm—'told someone, who told someone else, who let it be known to the police, that there's a voodoo on it.' He laughed.

'Or in it.' The girl laughed. 'My name's Victoria,' she said. 'What's yours?'

We introduced ourselves.

'Do you ever drive it?' Josh, I could see, was checking.

'We did, but we can't afford to tax it any more.'

'Would you hire it if we got it taxed?' I asked.

'Sure, but who to and what for?' Edward thought we were joking. 'It's nice for the cats, that's all. Your grandfather's old cat used to frolic about with the Siamese from the papershop.'

'She's had a kitten,' I said. 'It nearly killed her; she's twelve.'

'We heard. David told us; said she wasn't well. She all right now?'

'We met him. Yes, she's fine.' Josh was measuring them in his mind. 'Would you and your friend David rent the van? We are moving to the country. Grandpa says why don't we all go—he's coming, too—in your van, if you'll take us.'

Victoria and Edward stared. 'Who are you?' Victoria said. 'I've seen you somewhere.'

'We met yesterday at Pa's exhibition.'

'So we did, but you looked different.'

'Well, Pa's shy. You called him "Reverend". We were incognito,' I explained.

'The guy in the funny hat, your father, is he the painter?'

'Yes. It's not a funny hat, it's a Panama. It's funny in another way, it's—'

'Josh,' I warned.

'How do you mean? How funny?'

'Pa threw the television out of the window,' I said

desperately. 'He hates television and "progress". He's an artist. He's being driven mad in Croydon, that's why we are moving. We've bought a house with the money he got from his pictures—' I paused. Why was I telling our business to total strangers?

'He put all the money on a horse,' said Josh boastfully, 'and it won. He bought Haphazard House where we're going. Will you take us, and will your friend help with the van?'

'Why not? We all have to move.' Edward sounded unsurprised. 'Did your father paint your teeth blue?'

'No,' I said indignantly.

'I only meant that if he is a painter who chucks televisions around he might have a go at your teeth.'

'Well, I'm blowed!' Pa had crept up on us from behind. 'Here's the pin in Newton's eye.' He shook hands with Victoria. 'And who are you, really?'

'A furniture-removing team,' said Edward. 'Your kids are hiring us.'

'And will you do it?' Pa seemed to like the look of Edward and Victoria.

'The van isn't taxed; otherwise it's no problem.'

'What problem can't be solved?' said Pa. He was looking at Victoria as a suitable model, weighing up the contrast of flowing skirts and angular elbows.

'A holiday in the country,' she said. 'Super! The last we had was in a grotty place in Portugal where we got diarrhoea and nearly died. That's where we met David and bought the van. No more "abroad" for us now we have Baby.'

'We have a baby,' explained Edward.

'One baby won't make much odds. There are four of us and my father,' said Pa.

'And Bogus,' I said. 'And Old X-ray and her kitten.'

'We should all fit in all right.' Pa looked very pleased. 'By the way, would you like to come to supper? My wife seems to think we should stay the night and keep an eye on Old X-ray. She sent me out to buy food, so why don't you come, too? Only makes two more.' I had never seen Pa so expansive to strangers.

Victoria gave Edward's arm a little tweak. 'Say yes. May we bring Baby? He's called Arnold.'

'Arnold!' Pa looked aghast. 'What a name!'

'It's a family name. We just call him Baby.'

'Then bring him.'

'Thanks, we will.' They moved away, Victoria taking long strides in her trailing skirt, Edward hurrying to keep up with his short, thick legs.

'Now then, you two.' Pa sat down abruptly on the kerb. 'I have to talk to you.' He paused.

'Go ahead,' said Josh encouragingly, folding his legs under him and sitting beside Pa. The pause lengthened.

'Go on,' I said, standing above them. One could sit anywhere in the country, I thought. Pa, when he stood up, might find he'd been sitting on some bubblegum or worse. 'Go on, do,' I said.

'Sit down, then.'

I crouched beside them, an inch above the pavement. Bogus lolled indolently against the railings.

'It's—' said Pa. 'Well, it's—oh Lord, it's so *ridiculous*. It's the hat! I mean, it's mad, it's illogical, but your mother and grandfather and I, well—um—we all—um—think—'

'Know,' said Josh quietly.

'The animals know,' I said.

'Well, if you all know I needn't explain.' Pa looked relieved. 'We've got ourselves a magic hat and there it is.'

'Yes,' we said.

'Well then, let's go and buy some supper. We had better keep it quiet or we will find ourselves psychoanalysed or something. All we do is keep our traps shut until we take refuge in this Haphazard House, if it exists.'

'Oh, it exists.' Josh got up, smacking the dust from his bottom. 'We all saw its specification in writing, didn't we?'

'Never believe all you read,' said Pa, rising up tall.

'Shall we tell Victoria and Edward?' I asked.

'No, no, no. They might not trust us with the van.'

'What about the lad, David?' Josh liked calling people older than himself 'lad'.

'No, certainly not, he might think we were liars, to say the least.' And Pa began to sing to an improvised tune, 'Liars, lyres, tooraliah.'

'I think,' said Josh as we headed for the supermarket, 'I think he is afraid of getting out of its orbit. He can't wear it while Old X-ray is in it and he's not brave enough to go home without it, so we stay the night.'

'What are you two whispering about?' Pa called from the corner of the street. 'Lies to the sound of a lyre,' he sang.

Chapter 10

By the time Old X-ray's kitten opened its eyes, Pa had taxed the van and got Edward, who was practical, to check the engine. Grandpa gave his kitchen utensils and furniture to the squatters who were moving elsewhere. In Croydon Pa ordered that we travel light. Ma ruthlessly stripped us of all our possessions.

'I want,' she said, 'to have nothing to remember Croydon by.' Now that we were leaving, we admitted none of us had ever been happy there.

Pa, wearing the hat which Old X-ray had left after one night, settled up with our landlords, paid bills and packed his painting things.

Bogus was the only member of the family who, having nothing to do, was able to lounge about watching. He seemed better able than anyone to grasp a situation none of us was prepared to discuss. We had bought Haphazard House. We had made three new friends—Victoria, Edward and David; if you counted Baby, four. As soon as we were ready we would all travel west in the Mini and the painted van. There was little discussion, somehow—it seemed better not. We decided to start at dawn. Josh and I had washed and polished the van. Pa repainted some of the daisies and added some buttercups. We tidied up the Mini. Both vehicles were full of petrol and the tyres checked.

From their basement Victoria helped David bring four brass figures which they screwed into sockets at the corners of the van's roof. The first was of a girl in flimsy draperies, trailing a garland of flowers. Next a fat lady, arms folded across her chest, in the 'They shall not pass' attitude of French war memorials. Then Death carrying a scythe, and a dancing Harlequin. Edward fetched a rag and some Brasso and gave them an energetic polish.

David grinned at our surprised faces. 'This van was a hearse when I bought her. Nothing like a repaint job.' He ran a friendly hand over the floral work. 'Be back as soon as I can.' He ran off.

'Home, and we've never seen it,' I said to Josh who looked at me strangely, about to speak, but changed his mind.

'You must rest,' said Ma, passing us on her way up to Grandpa. 'We have far to go and need all our strength. The journey may be terrible. Lend me the hat, Andrew. You can't wear it all the time.' She took the hat; Pa parted with it reluctantly. 'A dawn start will save us all the holiday traffic hassle,' she said, pressing the hat on to her head and closing her eyes. 'That's better.' She handed me the hat. 'Take it in turns,' she said as she left us.

Victoria, with Baby asleep in her arms, came along the pavement with Edward. They sat on the steps without speaking, and we watched Pa pacing the street.

'I can't rest,' said Josh. 'I feel something might go wrong. There's an ominous feel in the air. Don't you feel it? Ominous.'

'Oh, shut up,' I said, and passed him the hat. 'Your turn.'

'Mine next.' Victoria was nervous. Edward put his arm round her. 'Silly,' he said gently. 'It's a *holiday*.' He pressed his bushy face close to hers so that his beard tickled her nose.

She sneezed; laughed apologetically. 'Something might go wrong,' she whispered. Josh handed the hat to Edward who held it above their two heads, smiling.

'Where is David?' I asked anxiously.

'Gone to fetch his girlfriend,' chorused Victoria and Edward.

'There isn't room for another person.' Josh looked worried. 'As it is we shall be a tight fit. He never said—'

'Here he comes,' Victoria exclaimed as David rounded the corner of the street walking fast. 'Got her?' she cried.

'Yes.' David looked triumphant. 'They never count heads accurately.'

'What's he on about? He hasn't got anyone with him. David, they say you're bringing a girl. There isn't room for anyone else. Pa said it's a tight fit.'

David stood looking up at us on the steps. He put his hand carefully into his pocket and held it palm upwards with a white mouse in it.

'There's room for Mouse,' he said and stroked the mouse with his finger. The mouse sniffed towards us, twitching her nose, whisking her whiskers in curiosity, then began to wash her ears with brisk movements of her paws. In the lamplit street the little animal looked ghostly, her pink eyes catching the light like tiny torches.

'I've stolen her.' David sat beside me carefully. 'I've been working for a hospital. The people use mice for experiments. Mouse has had four families, all gone.'

'Disgusting,' I said. 'I'd rather die than Mouse.' I felt anger.

'That's as may be. Vivisection's not nice. Mice don't ask to help humanity. I've grown very fond of this particular mouse and decided she shall have a natural death.'

'She won't have a nice death if she meets Old X-ray.' Josh peered at the mouse who was looking about her with interest.

'That's where you're wrong.' David put the mouse into his pocket. 'This mouse terrifies cats.'

'Tell us another,' Josh jeered.
David smiled. 'You wait and see.'
The stuffy night seemed to go on for ever. The pubs closed. People and cars grew fewer. The great orchestra of London faded to a rumble; its menacing noise jollied by the occasional blast of a police car. Some sleepless person let a radio play till it went off the air. Pa stopped his restless pacing and joined us to sit on the steps.
'The street air is stale. It smells,' Josh grumbled.
'Tomorrow will be different,' I said.
'You are looking very pretty, Miss Pin,' said Pa. He had lately taken to calling Victoria 'Miss Pin' in memory of our first meeting. 'Where, by the way, are those thick glasses?'
'Those are my picture-show glasses. I wear them to minimize the shock.'
Pa looked uncertain whether to take offence. David laughed, stroking Mouse gently.
'It's just her way,' said Edward, taking Baby from Victoria. 'Isn't it, Baby? Your mum's a funny girl.' Baby began to dribble on Edward's beard. 'She doesn't need glasses.' Pa looked suspicious. 'It's just her way.'
'Is everybody ready?' Ma came out with Grandpa carrying Old X-ray and the kitten, Angelique.
'Yes,' we all cried, springing to our feet. 'Yes, we are,' we answered joyfully. Whatever had been stalking the streets paused. The dawn was a gleam in the east bringing hope, fending off fear.
A sudden yell from Grandpa and Old X-ray flashed past and was gone.
'Oh no!' Ma cried. 'Oh no!' she wailed. 'Who let her out of the basket?'
'Oh my Lord!' David pocketed Mouse. 'Which way did she go?'
'It's still dark, she may be quite close. If everybody would stop making such a noise—'
'Stop the row, it will only frighten her more.' Grandpa,

trembling with anger, stood small and old on the pavement. 'She isn't used to going out.'

We looked under the Mini and the van. We looked under all the cars in the street. No Old X-ray.

'Puss, puss, puss,' called Victoria.

'She hates being called Puss,' shouted Grandpa.

'Don't shout, Grandpa, you'll scare her.'

'I'll shout if I want to. She's my cat. She likes me shouting.'

'Surely she will turn up,' said David.

'Nothing sure about it.' Grandpa, in the half-light, looked wizened with anxiety.

'What shall we do?' Josh asked.

'Keep calm,' Ma answered. 'The most difficult thing in the world.'

We stood on the doorstep and conferred. We decided that Grandpa, with the kitten, should wait on the doorstep while we searched.

I had never realized until that morning what a lot of cats there were in Grandpa's neighbourhood. Black cats, white cats, tabbies, gingers, Siamese, all out and about in the streets, but no sign of Old X-ray, no sign whatever; and nobody had seen her, not the milkman, the postman, nor the police.

'What does it look like?' people asked.

'A calico cat: tortoiseshell with black ears, white tummy, golden eyes, white face.'

'No,' they said. 'Sorry.' And went about their business.

It grew light and the streets filled. We came back to Grandpa to check, but each time he just shook his head. 'No sign,' he said. Angelique, becoming hungry, mewed.

After my sixth search I came back to find a small crowd gathered around Grandpa. My spirits soared but soon fell. Someone had asked him what we were all doing. Why were we leaving London?

'To bury ourselves in the country. To get away from the

noise, the people, the smells, the aggression. If it were not for that cat we would be well on our way.' Pa was desperate.

'I shan't leave. Wild horses won't move me. We should have known the portents. False Start, indeed!' Grandpa suddenly nipped back through the front door, slammed it and was gone, cat basket and all. David came along the street. I saw Victoria speak anxiously to him. Usually so calm, he clutched his head, then threw up his arms and flung back his head like some medieval martyr. He remained in that attitude, his finger pointing. High above our heads, looking down from the parapet of the house, peered Old X-ray, her eyes yellow in the morning sun, her ears back, pink nose querying. Very slowly she stretched down a tentative paw then withdrew it. Above us the top window opened and Grandpa, white faced, stared down at us.

'Look out!' cried Josh, as Old X-ray sprang, landing neatly on his head, scrambling along his back into the flat.

'She has nine lives.' Ma was weeping with laughter. 'We had forgotten that.'

'I had not.' Pa inserted himself behind the wheel of the Mini.

'It was my fault. I'm sorry.' David spoke confidentially to Ma. 'The cat must have seen Mouse. Sit quiet now,'—he patted a small bulge in his pocket—'or you'll be causing more trouble.'

'Hurry,' shouted Pa from the Mini. 'Hurry. We are late.' He started the engine.

A chill wind blew down the street filling me with fear. The others were affected, too. We pushed Grandpa with his cats into the van. Victoria, looking pale, clambered in carrying Baby. Edward and David slammed the doors. David got behind the wheel. As Josh got into the Mini, Bogus leapt in with the hat in his jaws. Pa snatched it and put it on. 'Follow,' Pa called to David, 'follow me.' David shouted something and waved his arm. Sitting on the back seat with Bogus pressed against me I heard a voice calling, 'Lisa, Lisa,' but the street was empty when I looked back. I could have sworn it was the voice I had thought I heard at Mr Heath's, the dentist.

We drove through the afternoon into the evening and into the night until we stopped in the square of a sleeping village and Pa said in a voice I had never heard before,

'This is Coldharbour.'

Chapter 11

Stillness. We gathered close together in the road. I had never experienced stillness. The quiet was awesome. My tired ears, full of the sound of traffic and the Mini's engine, took a while to adjust.

Then I heard the cooling engines click, and Victoria sigh. There was a full moon. The shadow of a church tower fell across our group. The church clock ticked, the minute hand jerked, the clock whirred, then struck twice.

The square was small; four roads led from it. On tiptoe Josh and I explored. There was a post office and general store, and that was all in the way of shops. The village was very small, the church of cathedral proportions. We went back to the others.

'Which way now?' Even Grandpa didn't speak above a whisper.

'I don't know.' Pa tipped the hat to the back of his head.

'We cannot wake anybody at this hour,' whispered Ma.

'Why not?' Grandpa looked worn out.

'Darling, just look at us.' Ma grinned. I could see her teeth in the moonlight. 'We'd make an awful impression. We look like a pop festival in this van. Or refugees.'

'Maybe, but we must ask where Haphazard is. We can't spend the rest of the night here.' Pa spoke reasonably enough.

'Doesn't the—' I began.

'No, it *doesn't*,' Pa hissed. He tipped the hat forward. '*Nothing*.'

'Oh.' I felt betrayed. I believed magic worked best at night. With this moon the night was magical.

'Look!' Edward spoke low. 'What's wrong with your dog?'

Bogus was leaping about, jumping and bowing, his ears flapping, tail wagging, he growled and whined throatily. He ran a little way down the road and looked back.

'That creature wants us to follow it.' Grandpa spoke emphatically. Bogus pranced back then ran off again to look back, invitingly. From the van Old X-ray dropped down to the road and, with tail high, went leaping to join Bogus. The two animals set off side by side.

'Push the cars down the slope, then we won't wake the village.' Pa scrambled into the Mini and Ma gave it a shove, then jumped in as it moved.

Victoria gave the van a heave, helped by Josh. We rolled down the slope clear of the village before starting the engine.

Ahead, Bogus and Old X-ray trotted, Bogus steadily, Old X-ray in the manner of cats, in dashes and stops. After a while the animals stopped and Old X-ray jumped back into the van. Bogus quickened his pace, running hard, ears and tail streaming back. Josh and I sat with David in the van.

At a crossroads Bogus turned left. The road grew narrow. By the light of the moon I had my first glimpse of Haphazard: a low house, lying under a hill at the top of a valley on the far side of a wood.

'That's Haphazard. I recognize it.' Josh was crying.

'Josh, you're crying.'

'I'm not. I'm happy.' He wiped tears away with the back of his hand.

'It's a trick of the imagination,' said David. 'That house is hidden by the wood.'

'But you saw it, too.' I looked sidelong at David.

'Sure I did. I've worn that hat, haven't I?'

'Oh,' I said, digesting this fact.

We followed the Mini into the wood. 'Lovely wood!' I was excited. The wood was dark, mysterious, a wood we were to know later to be full of oak and beech, hazel and holly, here and there a wild cherry and at one end thickets of blackthorn and briar. The track wound twisting through the trees, dipping to a stream which we forded. Then we were out of the wood and had arrived. Looking up at the house, I thought somebody watched us from a window, but the moon went behind a cloud. When I looked again there was no one.

Bogus was battering at the door with his paws, whimpering, snuffling, growling.

'Who has the key?' Grandpa got down from the van, holding the kitten. Old X-ray wound herself in and out between his feet, purring and arching her back. 'I have,' said Ma and gave a clumsy key to Pa.

Pa put the key in the lock, turned it, pushed. The door swung open and we all crowded in.

Chapter 12

We walked into a long room with a stone floor. The moonlight pouring through the windows gave light. The walls were white and bare, the ceiling moulded; at the end of the room a large fireplace, a sofa on either side of it. Against the walls stood chairs and tables. There were doors in the inner wall. There was a smell of wood smoke. The effect in the moonlight was grey and muted white. Gentle.

One door led into another room, the walls lined with bookshelves. Above the fireplace hung a mirror which reflected our tired faces. There was ash in the grate. Oak chests stood against the wall, armchairs in the middle of the room; the windows looked into a cobbled courtyard.

A second door led into a cloakroom with a washbasin and lavatory in willow pattern. Ma pulled the chain and water rushed in an enthusiastic surge. 'That works, at least,' she said.

The third door led to a kitchen with a range such as I had seen in picture books, a tall dresser on which was a dinner service; pots and pans hung by the range.

'Nice job for somebody,' said Pa. 'They are copper.'

Beyond the kitchen was a scullery with a sink and wooden plate rack; in the corner a pump.

'Exercise for all.' Edward pumped, and below our feet water gurgled. Victoria turned on a tap and, after a few hiccups, water ran.

'How do we get upstairs? I want to go to bed.' Grandpa wheezed with fatigue. We looked for the stairs.

'In a house like this they would go up from the hall.'

We went back to the front of the house. Once the stairs had indeed gone up from here, but no more. The charred remains of a staircase went up the wall; no framework remained, just the black marks of fire.

'The fire was in 1949, the man said.' I remembered Squire, Close and Sword.

'Perhaps we were impetuous,' said Ma hesitantly.

'We can climb up,'—Josh pointed—'up here. Look.' Against the house grew a magnolia. Josh and I began to climb it. The branches were tough; shiny leaves clattered as we climbed.

'Oh,' I exclaimed, 'it's in flower.' I touched a white flower which nearly overpowered me with its scent. Josh forced a casement window and we were soon looking down at the others from where the head of the stairs had been.

'So I can't go to bed.' Grandpa was furious. He turned, left the house and climbed back into the van.

'Perhaps there are back stairs,' said Pa below us. We searched and found back stairs but they had many treads missing. 'These can be repaired.' David examined them.

'How many rooms are there? I'm coming up.' Pa began to climb. 'The first thing we must get is a ladder.' He manoeuvred himself in at the window.

We found the bedrooms, a large bathroom with a fireplace in it; the bath and lavatory had mahogany surrounds. Every bedroom was empty except one in which furniture was piled, all heaped higgledy-piggledy.

'Deal with that later. Let's get down and see what more there is.' We followed Pa down the magnolia. 'Haphazard it certainly is.' He jumped the last six feet to the ground.

'Andrew, come here,' Ma called. We followed Pa.

'Look,' said Ma. She was kneeling by the hearth in the hall. 'This fire is still warm. The ash is glowing.'

'How peculiar.' Pa held his hand over the ash. 'See whether you can find some wood,' he said to us. 'Look in the outhouses.'

We found logs by the back door and soon the fire in the hall was ablaze. Ma looked puzzled. 'Let's get the other fires going.'

In the room next to the hall the ash was easily lit. We brought Grandpa in and he fell asleep with the kitten, stretched out on a sofa. The rest of us unloaded the van and the Mini before they were driven round to the yard at the back of the house.

Josh and I explored, moving away from the house across the grass.

Josh pointed. 'That's the tree which hid one part of the house when I first saw it, when you and Pa came home with the hat.'

An enormous oak with spreading branches stood fifty yards from the house. A bit awed by its size, we stared. An owl cried in the wood and we watched as one, and soon another, flew across the space from the wood to the tree. 'They must live there.'

'Josh—'

'Yes?'

'Nothing.' I had nearly mentioned the person at the window.

The grass sloped down to the wood. I sat down. I was tired. The grass was soft; I closed my eyes and lay back. I did not sleep for long. A wren's loud song awoke me; a rabbit thumped its feet. Far off a cock crowed and I heard the church clock strike. I kept my eyes tight shut. This dream was too good to leave. I had never smelled anything in my dreams before.

'Has anyone seen Lisa?' my mother's voice called in the house.

'No,' voices answered. 'No.'

'Perhaps she went with your father.'

'No, he was alone.'

'Ask Bogus to find her.'

I listened sleepily to their voices. In the wood a cock pheasant let out a warning 'cackcack'. Bogus licked my face and scraped at my shoulder with his paw. I opened a reluctant eye and he snuffed.

'Oh, Bogus, such a dream!'

'Lisa,' Ma called.

'Coming.' I sat up. The sun was up and I was hungry. I followed Bogus to the house. There were sounds of activity. Someone was working the pump. David came round the house pushing a barrow full of logs. I smelt bacon and coffee and followed my nose to the kitchen. Ma, wearing an apron, was at the range frying bacon, making coffee, laughing and talking. She looked so happy I stopped in the doorway and stared.

'Lisa darling, come and have breakfast.'

'Ma.' I went and kissed her. 'Ma.'

'What is it?' she asked.

'I don't know. I can't say.' She handed me a plate of bacon and fried bread. 'Go and sit by your grandfather. Eat it before it gets cold.' Grandpa, a cup of coffee in his hands, gave me a sharp look from under beetle brows. His fingers looked like knotted hawthorn twigs.

'You don't know what a hawthorn looks like.' He spoke low. I blushed. 'Nor could you recognize a wren or a pheasant.'

'No,' I whispered.

'Then hush,' he said.
'What did you say?' asked Ma.
'I told Lisa to hush.'
'The poor child said nothing.'
'She was about to.'
'Really, you are unfair!' Ma exclaimed.
'Only taking precautions.'
Ma smiled and heaped a plate with food for David who had just come in. 'Hungry?'
'Starving.'
'Where's Pa?' I asked.
'Gone to the village.'
'Is he—has he got the hat?'
'No, it's hanging in the hall,' Grandpa hissed.
'Where are Edward and Victoria?'
'Exploring.'
'And Josh?'
'He's had breakfast; he's gone to the walled garden.'
'Oh, the walled garden. I'd forgotten there is one.'
'Yes,' said Grandpa, stroking Angelique who had scrambled up his leg, 'a fine walled garden. Somebody's cultivating it.'
'Who?'
'Your father will ask if he remembers. Now shut up.'
'Aren't you being a bit stiff with Lisa?' My mother looked annoyed.
'Cautious.' Grandpa gave her a benign smile. 'He will also, one hopes, bring a ladder. I can't climb magnolias, but I might manage a ladder until we get a staircase built.'
I ate my breakfast, wondering at Grandpa's knowledge and awareness.
'A circular stair would be nice,' said Ma, joining us to eat. 'I dreamt I bought one in a sale.'
'You dreaming too,' Grandpa looked at her suspiciously.
'Yes. You are not the only one to dream.'

Chapter 13

I left the house and set off to explore. The cobblestones of the yard humped under the soles of my feet. The painted van was under cover in a coach-house. It looked smaller than it had in London, the brass figures more relaxed than I had remembered. The fat woman looked contented and the figure of Death more like a man about to cut grass than life. During the journey the Harlequin had swung round in his socket to face the girl. I climbed up to put him straight but I could not move him.

A door in the wall led into the walled garden. I went through, closing it behind me. There were rows of vegetables, well tended, along the walls, fruit trees. I picked a peach and bit the sweet flesh, feeling the furry skin on my tongue as the juice ran down my chin. I listened. Blackbirds in the raspberry canes shrieked and flew away noisily; a bullfinch piped near me. There was a loud noise of insects; bees buzzed, flies hummed, butterflies on a buddleia rustled their wings like tissue paper. The garden centred on a well. I saw my face looking up from dark water. High above me a buzzard shrieked. I stood watching as he wheeled with his mate in the morning sky to disappear over a hill. At my feet there was a scraping sound; a large toad pulled one slow leg after the other, crossed the flagstones around the well to move out of sight into a clump of iris. My mind flew back to St James's Square and Mr Bailey sticking tickets under the windscreen-wipers of the rich, his heart full of longing. I left the garden by another door to find myself in the open behind the house. I climbed a slope to a point where I could look down. All the windows on the ground floor were open and presently I saw my mother, Victoria, David and Edward climb up the magnolia. I wondered where Grandpa could be and spied him sitting with his back to a tree with Old X-ray and Angelique sitting prim beside him.

Upstairs windows flew open and I heard my mother talking to the others. They were moving furniture and setting up beds. In the still air I could hear their feet shuffling as they carried heavy beds, then light as they ran from room to room. Not far from Grandpa a kestrel swept down to hover a few feet from the ground, before catching sight of Old X-ray and winging off. I wondered where Josh was and set out towards the wood to look.

The ground under the trees was springy, the sun pale green through the beeches. I found the stream and followed it. Fish darted in pools and a heron flew up, trailing long legs. I listened to the noise of the stream as it passed over stones, round rocks, cutting deep under high banks. Rounding a bend, I came on a long, deep pool, almost black at the edges and perfectly clear in the middle.

'Come in and swim.' Josh and Bogus were sitting on the opposite bank. 'It's quite warm. The water is marvellous; it's like swimming in beer.'

I undressed and dived in. I had never felt such water. After London's harsh product this was silk. I let my hair trail like weed. Josh joined me and we swam until we tired, then climbed out on the bank to sit by Bogus in the sun.

'I went up the hill through the wood,' said Josh. 'I followed the stream. It comes down the hill in falls, and in all the pools there are trout. I saw a fox. I've never seen one before.'

'There might well be,' I said.

'And badgers, I'm sure. There are lots of deep holes halfway up the hill. You must come and look.'

'I will.' I felt the sun drying my body and shook my wet hair.

'You know the garden, the walled garden?'

'Yes.'

'It's locked. I couldn't get in but I looked over the wall.'

'No, it isn't. I've just come from there.'

'The door is locked, silly you.'

'No, I'm not.'

'Very, very silly.'

I hated being called silly. 'I'm not. I've just been in there. I ate a peach.'

'Oh rot!' Josh mocked. I slapped his face. We fought, slipped and fell into the water. Bogus barked, bowing to us from the bank. I surfaced, my hair streaming over my eyes. I was furious.

'I'll show you. I've got the peach stone in my pocket.'

'You can buy peaches anywhere.'

'Come with me. There's a toad there, too.'

Josh came sulkily to the garden and stared. 'It must be another garden. This was locked.'

I said, 'If you look from up the hill you can see there's only one.'

Josh looked along the wall to the peach trees, went and picked one and bit. 'All right, now where's the toad?' He looked embarrassed.

'You look embarrassed,' I said, taunting.

'Well, I am. The door was locked against me. Why? It's not the sort of thing that happens every day.' He paused. 'I don't suppose it happened every day in fairy stories.'

'We are too old for fairy stories,' I said. We ate more peaches, thoughtfully. 'Shall we take some to the house?' We picked the fruit and put it in rhubarb leaves.

'Did you notice Bogus last night?' Josh pushed open the door to the yard.

'Didn't we all?'

'Nobody commented.' Josh patted Bogus. 'Nobody said nuffink, did they Bogus?' Bogus wagged his tail.

'Oh look,' said Josh, as we came round the front of the house, 'here comes Pa with one of the village lads and a ladder. Now Grandpa can get up to bed.'

We watched Pa drive up in the Mini followed by a truck with a ladder in the back. The driver was a grizzled man in blue jeans with a beret on the back of his head. He had blue eyes set in a brown face. Bogus went up to him, wagging his tail.

''Ullo, 'ullo, if it isn't Rags! 'Ullo, boy, where 'ave you been then?'

Chapter 14

'This is Mr Pearce, darling. He is very kindly lending us a ladder.' Pa introduced Mr Pearce to our mother who shook his hand. 'It's very kind of you, Mr Pearce, to help us.'

'Well, you have to get upstairs.' Mr Pearce looked down at Ma. 'I hear you climbed the magnolia; won't do it no good to do that.'

'No. It's such a beautiful tree, it must be very old.'

'Not all that old.' Mr Pearce let go of Ma's hand. 'It was sickly until the fire, then the fire set it up!'

'How?' I asked.

'Magnolias like heat. When the stairs burned the walls grew hot and the magnolia pulled herself together and grew. But she won't like you climbing up and down her.'

'We'll use the ladder.' Ma tried to reassure.

Mr Pearce forced his eyes away from Ma's and took a long look at Josh, then me, then Grandpa, his eyes large, blue, unblinking. 'This all of you?'

'All the Fullers. I told you about our three friends.' Pa was enjoying the inspection.

'So you did. Well, let's set up the ladder.' Mr Pearce started to untie the rope which held it. 'This should do you.' He eased it to the ground. 'Funny you should have brought Rags along with you.' He fondled Bogus's head.

'He's called Bogus.' Josh was polite.

'He was Rags when he left.'

'When was that?' Ma asked.

'After Mr Hayco died, after the fire. Hung about a bit, poor dog, then he left. Wouldn't live with nobody else, would you Rags?' Bogus wagged his tail.

'But you said the fire was in 1949. Bogus can't be Rags; it's nearly forty years.'

'Forty or so,' agreed Mr Pearce.

'A long time,' said Pa.

'Time's a funny thing. This is Rags.'

'Well,' said Pa in the awkward silence which followed this statement, 'let's see how the ladder goes.'

The ladder reached from the hall to the landing. Mr Pearce fixed the foot with a heavy wood block and wedged it at the top. 'There,' he said to Grandpa, 'you try it.'

Grandpa climbed halfway up with agility followed by Old X-ray and Bogus. They squeezed past him. Grandpa hesitated.

'Can't do it. Won't do it,' Grandpa grunted.

'Go on, Father, you are doing fine,' Pa called from below.

'I'm not ready.' Grandpa lowered himself down the ladder, clutching the rungs as though he were afraid of falling. 'Not ready.' I got the impression he was not so much afraid of the ladder as of reaching the top. There was something up there he was afraid of. I met his eyes as he reached my side. 'Not afraid, just not ready,' he muttered.

'Who is up there, Grandpa? D'you know who it is?'

He looked sly. 'Don't know what you're talking about.' I didn't believe him. The others were all watching Bogus and Old X-ray.

'Rags was always good up the ladders, used to come up the hayricks. Lots of dogs can climb ladders, but Rags, he doesn't mind coming down. That's what makes him different, ain't it boy?' said Mr Pearce looking up.

Bogus peered at the ladder then came down without hesitation. Mr Pearce laughed. 'Now Mr Hayco's nephew what sold this house, he never thought to borrow a ladder.'

'What did he do?' David had joined us, coming quietly into the house.

'Stayed for a few days, liked it not and left.'

'Liked it not and died,' murmured David.

'But he didn't die, did he? Put the place on the market.'

'Lucky for us,' I said.

'Maybe.' Mr Pearce gave the ladder a shake to make sure it was firm.

'What do you mean, "Maybe"?' I asked curiously.

'Maybe. Well, maybe if you come to terms?'

'Come to terms?'

'That's what I said.' Mr Pearce spoke rather smugly I

thought. Ma invited him inside. He followed her into the kitchen. 'A cup of tea?' asked Ma.

'Thank you.' Mr Pearce sat down at the table and looked at the range. 'You don't want to be bothered with that range,' he said. 'What you need is an Aga.'

'Need?' Ma grinned complicitly. 'I can manage with this, Mr Pearce.' Mr Pearce smiled at Ma. Ma filled the kettle, smiling. 'The front stairs—that's different.'

'I can fix the back stairs for you.'

'How so?' Grandpa had come to join us.

'Very expensive, if you don't stay.' Mr Pearce's eyes met mine, then glanced away.

'But of course we shall stay, stay for ever.' I spoke angrily.

'Steady on,' said Mr Pearce. 'Steady on, my beauty.'

'I thought—' Pa was lounging in the doorway, wearing the hat. 'I thought just now when we put the ladder up how beautiful it would be to have a spiral stair made of glass. It would give an elegant dimension.'

'How did you know?' Mr Pearce gave a sudden roar. 'Who told you? That stair was his, his great idea, not yours—not—not—not—yours. NO.'

There was a long, awkward pause. I felt very frightened.

'I don't think I can tell you because I'm not sure I know, but I think I have come to terms.' Pa spoke softly. 'Could you tell us where the staircase is?'

'Oh, Mr Pearce!' Ma gave a cry. 'Oh, Mr Pearce, don't.' She rushed across the kitchen. 'Please don't cry.' Tears were oozing from his blue eyes.

'I thought you'd never come. It's a shock.' Mr Pearce gulped. 'An 'orrible shock, *'orrible*.' Ma wiped Mr Pearce's eyes with a corner of her apron.

'Catch the aitch, Mr P.,' she cried boldly. 'Here,' she snatched the hat from Pa's head. 'Wear this for a few minutes and you'll find it all tumbles into place, whatever it is.' She put the hat on Mr Pearce's head and her arm round his shaking shoulders. We were watching this scene when Victoria, wearing her long skirt and bean beads, strode into the room, followed by Edward. 'Give me my specs,' she exclaimed. 'This I have to see. The poor man's hurt. There, there,' she said. 'Don't cry. Please don't.'

Victoria's arms were full of lilies, large cream flowers, spotted with brown, their stamens heavy with yellow pollen.

'Where did you find those?' Mr Pearce, the tears wet on his cheeks, stared at Victoria as though she were an apparition.

'Growing in the wood.' Victoria laid the flowers on the table, her beads making a gritty noise as they swung against her chest. 'There are lots of them and the smell is fantastic.'

'I should get them out of the house if I was you, double quick.'

'Oh.' Victoria handed the flowers to me. 'Why?'

'They won't do no good. They don't belong to the house.'

Victoria looked at Mr Pearce doubtfully, then she took Baby from Edward and held him out to Mr. Pearce.

'Like to hold him?' Mr Pearce took Baby. ''Ello, 'ello, 'ello,' he said, 'if it ain't young Arnold.'

'Mr Pearce—' Only Ma was brave enough to speak. 'How do you know his name is Arnold?'

'It is, isn't it?'

'Yes,' said Victoria, taking off the pebble glasses through which she had been staring at Mr Pearce and straightening up so that the beads clattered. 'But we call him Baby most of the time.'

Our visitor tossed Baby up and down on his knee and took stock of Victoria. After a time he said, 'If you stay and think of getting the garden back in order, you might plant them beans.' He stretched out a hand and fingered the necklace.

'But it *is*,' Josh and I chorused. 'It is in order.'

'Nay.'

'Yeah!'

'Nay.'

'Yeah!'

'What's this? A Bible class?' Grandpa had been silent up to now.

'Garden was famous once.'

'The garden's in perfect order,' I said.

'Nay!'

'Yeah, Mr Pearce. There are beans, peas, spinach and a toad.'

'Somebody's kept it in order then,' said Pa.

'Nobody would. People don't come here much.'

'Why not?'

'Well—' He drew out the word.

'Because it is haunted, I suppose,' I said.

Mr Pearce looked uncomfortable.

'A useful ghost.' Pa looked cheerful. 'Left warm ash in the fireplace, and digs the garden.'

'That so,' Mr Pearce handed Baby back to Victoria. 'Those lilies should go—they ain't for you,' he said. 'I must be going or Mrs Pearce will give me stick.' He shook hands with Ma and, giving the rest of us a wave, drove off.

'Who is he?' Ma watched the van vanish into the wood.

'Local builder,' said Pa. 'He says.'

'Funny he should know both Bogus and Baby.'

'Baby looks like most babies and there are lots of mongrels like Bogus.'

'No, love, there are not. And Bogus knew him; he greeted him.'

'He knows a lot,' I said. 'Mr Pearce and Bogus, too.' I stroked the silky ears. 'If Bogus could talk he could sort out everything for us.'

'Pity he left so soon. I wanted to ask about the stairs.' Pa looked thoughtful. 'He seemed to imply that there are stairs, glass stairs.'

'He seems to be in a bit of a muddle. Bogus, Baby, whether we are staying. Why doesn't he expect us to stay?' Ma looked at Pa.

'Possibly we won't be able to.' He smiled at her then gave her a kiss. 'Don't worry, darling. This is different from

London. Let's get settled in. I've found a splendid loft to work in, quiet, with the right light. That's a great blessing.' Ma smiled, a little sadly.

'We've escaped,' said Pa. 'The noise, the crowds, the smell, the traffic, the people, the violence, Father's fear of eviction, the terrible hurry, the aggression, the dreary existence.'

'School,' said Josh.

'You'll have to go to school here.' Ma was brisk. 'You aren't in quarantine for imaginary measles any more. No doubt there's a school.'

As I came down to reality with a bump, I wondered whether the person I had seen at the window when we arrived would stay on with us. Whether he/she was of school age like us, or like Baby and Bogus seemed to be to Mr Pearce—ageless.

'May I borrow the hat please? I want to see whether I really saw a toad in the garden.' I looked at Pa.

'You'll see them at night, but by all means try.'

'We must write to Mr Bailey,' I said.

'Perhaps Mr Pearce knows him, too.' Ma seemed to be accepting Mr Pearce with serenity.

I shivered as I put the hat on. Everything seemed out of focus, and I was frightened. I wondered how Haphazard House had got its name and what the hazards were. The sky was overcast. I took the lilies into the yard, wondering what to do with them. She shouldn't have picked them, I thought. It would have been better to leave them growing. A bucket lay on its side by a tap. I righted it and turned on the tap. The scent of the flowers was fearfully strong. I put them in the bucket. Perhaps Mr Pearce had meant the smell was too strong indoors, that it would give Baby snivels. I arranged the flowers.

In the coach-house David's van looked young and jolly though it was almost a vintage machine. The four figures on the corners of the roof shone in the gloom. Bending to arrange the flowers, the hat tipped foward over my nose. I picked up the bucket, climbed on the van's bonnet and pushed it to the centre of the roof. The lilies looked right up there. I went on my way.

When I reached the garden it was silent and there were no toads to be seen. I sat down and listened to the silence, my heart uneasy. I laid the hat beside me and stared at the clump of iris into which the toad had crawled. The flowers were over and the seed pods bursting with red fruit. As I sat studying the jointed stalks and the butcher's knife leaves, I heard the clink of a hoe working through the earth and the breathing of a man working, breathing which now and again became a low whistle ending with a cough and a sniff. I hoped the man who kept this wonderful garden would not mind our intrusion. I stood up to introduce myself but there was nobody there. Snatching up the hat I ran.

Chapter 15

I raced into the house to shout 'Ma!' but terror made me dumb. I stopped by the door to listen and put the hat on the hatstand. There was nobody on the ground floor. I ran from room to room, each one still and empty. I scrambled up the ladder from the hall trying to call out for Ma. My voice was a tremulous bleat, 'Ma-a-a.'

'Everybody's out.'

David lay on the landing floor facing the wall. I could see his feet, bare, rather dirty and his foreshortened body at the top of the ladder. 'Don't be so noisy,' he said irritably.

'What are you doing?' Though not my mother, David was a person I knew. I felt better, less panicky.

'Hush. Can't you be quiet. I am launching Mouse.'

'Launching?'

'That's what I said.' By David's hand Mouse crouched, twitching, and hesitating, whiskers bristling, her ears alert.

Presently she moved, stretching out her body towards the wainscot, every nerve strained.

'Oh,' I said. 'I see.'

'Interesting,' David stated.

'Not very.' My heart still thumped. Fear made me rude. How could a white mouse compare with an invisible gardener?

David lay still. Mouse, on a level with his nose, remained for a few moments then, at some secret signal, she moved her tiny feet, scratching on the boards, and vanished into a crack in the wainscot. David sat up. 'There,' he said happily. 'She never thought that could happen to her.'

'Why not?' I sat beside him. My breath came normally now. It was safe sitting by David with his bare feet and torn jeans.

'She was bred for experiments, not to have fun. She can try her own experiments here.'

'Won't she be missed?'

'Possibly.' His voice was flat.

'So she'll become a house mouse,' I liked David a lot.

'She will.' David sat up and looked at me. 'What's been happening to you? You look het-up.'

I told him about the invisible gardener. I spoke as lightly as I could. 'It's nothing really, not as important as Mouse. I was frightened. I expect you will laugh.'

'No I won't. It's a bit like Mouse. Now you see her, now you don't, but she's there in that wall and your sniffing gardener is there, too. You heard him. Let's make some tea.' We climbed down the ladder.

'I shall put food up there for her until she can fend for herself.' David's thoughts were with Mouse. 'She'll have a life of adventure.'

I pictured Mouse exploring the secrets behind the walls of the house.

'Where are all the others?'

'They went to the village to check on the time and so on.'

'Ma and Pa have watches.'

David looked pitying. 'Time.' He stressed the word. 'They've gone to meet the village, find the shops, find their feet, find a school for you. What's known as "high time".' He laughed.

'Or time to know better. Why?'

'They were rattled by friend Pearce.'

'What he said about Bogus and Baby and the stairs?'

'Right, and an Aga instead of the range.'

'That sort of time? Modern?'

'Right again.'

'Why didn't you go, too?'

'I don't give much for time. My hold is tenuous. Any time suits me.'

'What do you mean?' We had reached the kitchen and David was filling the kettle while I pumped the water.

'Your Grandpa's time, your Ma and Pa's time are all different. Take Mouse, her time's short, your Grandpa's long. Time used to be pretty steady—it isn't now.'

'It's not steady *here*,' I heard myself say. David glanced at me, warmed the pot, put in tea, poured on boiling water. 'People feel they have to check on Greenwich Mean Time,' he said, 'to start with.'

'I don't understand.' I took the cup he handed me. I felt uneasy again.

'Keep your cool. No need to get scared.'

'I'm not, not really.'

'Don't make me laugh. You're as scared as Mouse but she's making use of her time. You'll be okay if you do, too.'

I warmed my hands round the cup. David sat silent. He had said all he had to say. I went and sat on the front step and waited for my family in the sun. Within reach of the hatstand I felt safe and calm though I had had the hat with me when I had been so frightened. Along the front of the house clumps of thyme and lavender grew between the flagstones, sweet alyssum gave off whiffs of scent. I got up to explore. Growing against the house, as well as the magnolia we had climbed, were roses and jasmine rising from a froth of Mediterranean daisies. The house was roofless where the fire had destroyed it. In the ruins grew buddleias and syringa, a self-sown garden with butterflies and bees feeding on clumps of Michaelmas daisies. It was very peaceful. I decided to find the room from which we had been watched when we arrived. David lay on a sofa in the hall, reading. If I shrieked he would hear me. I climbed the ladder and walked from room to room. My mother had done marvels. Beds were ready, chests of drawers, cupboards, chairs set about. Mirrors shone, wood glowed, rugs and carpets were soft underfoot, no spiders' webs, no dust, no smears.

I wandered from room to room guessing which one was whose. The bedrooms all opened on to a passage; it was more proper to call it a gallery. This must be for Grandpa I supposed, and this, with a fourposter, Ma and Pa's. Josh's room had his jeans and shirt lying on the floor. This room, also with a canopied bed, mine, as Bogus's basket was in a corner—a token, since he usually slept across my feet. 'For form's sake,' Pa had remarked when Ma bought the basket in the Portobello Road.

In another room Baby's things were neatly arranged, and Victoria's bean necklaces on the bedside table. Two more rooms—David's, and another ready for a guest. If Mr Bailey would desert his post and visit us he would be happy.

I remembered the watcher and went to find the window above the front door. However, whichever window I looked out of was either to the left of the porch or the right. There was no room above the porch, no window from which to observe. I felt teased and angry, the more so as Old X-ray and Angelique followed me from one room to another, purring, waving contented tails. I gave up and leant out of the window of Ma and Pa's room, looking across at the wood. The cats jumped up on the sill and sat, blinking. I listened to clocks ticking and furniture creaking in the house and the sounds of birds and insects, so different from the noises of London, usually full of menace.

My family came out of the wood: Pa, Ma, Victoria

carrying Baby, Edward and Josh, their arms full of parcels, Grandpa and Bogus strolling slowly. I went to meet them, running, my heart light.

'Poor old Mini gave her last gasp as we reached the village,' said Pa, bending to kiss me. I was horrified. We had had Mini ever since I could remember. 'From now on Shanks's Pony,' said Pa.

'Who was that with you at the window?' asked Victoria.

'The *next* window; she had the cats with her,' Josh corrected her.

'I was alone,' I said.

'Don't be silly. He was wearing the hat and he waved like this.' Josh made a regal gesture rather like the Queen Mother but more hearty.

'David?' Pa asked casually.

'I was alone,' I repeated.

'He was leaning out of the window above the porch, stupid.'

I stared at Josh, my insides churning. 'There isn't one. David's downstairs and the hat's on the hatstand.' I felt resentment as well as fear.

They said, 'Ah' thoughtfully, looking kindly at me.

'Did you find out the time in the village?' I wanted to change the subject.

'Yes.' Pa's voice was reassuring. 'Plenty of time to get settled before school starts, if it starts.' I felt time swinging down round my shoulders like a hoop.

'The school must be in another village,' said Ma.

'Grandpa found time to buy a false nose,' said Josh, 'in the shop.'

'He rides his jokes to death, let's hope this one doesn't last as long as poor Mini.' Ma sighed.

'I heard you.' Grandpa came up to us. 'I'm hardly likely to last as long as that machine, however cruelly you drive me.'

'Darling.' Ma looked at Grandpa with affection. The ruts and creases of his face crinkled into a grin.

'Give me some of your parcels.' I took them from her. 'Ma, I must speak to you.'

'All right.'

Grandpa walked on towards the house, bald head, shapeless jersey, old flannel trousers. 'So like the hind legs of an elephant.' Ma, watching him, was loving.

'Ma.' I laid my hand on her arm.

'Yes, What's bothering you?'

'There's someone working in the walled garden. I can hear him but I can't see him.'

'Really?'

'Yes. I was scared to death. I ran.'

'You mustn't be frightened, you really must not.'

'But I was. I am.'

'Listen.' Ma sat down on the grass, giving it a little pat so that I sat beside her. 'Listen to me. This morning we went up and sorted the furniture upstairs, the beds and so on.'

'I know. I heard and saw you.'

'We sorted the furniture into different rooms, beds, chairs, chests of drawers and so on, and then came down to the kitchen and had coffee. Then David, Edward and Victoria went out.'

'So?'

'I went up again to sort out sheets and blankets and—'

'And?'

'I found—'Ma gave a helpless shrug—'the furniture had all been rearranged, the beds were made up, the floors, the furniture, the windows were polished; it had all been very dusty but suddenly it was spotless. So when you tell me there is an invisible gardener I accept it.'

'Weren't you frightened?'

'Why should I be? It is a good thing and the furniture looks happy.'

'Furniture happy?'

'Furniture can look absolutely furious if you put it in the wrong place. It knows where it belongs.'

'It can't polish and dust itself.'

'One had always imagined so.' Ma stood up. 'Come on.'

I told her about David's mouse.

'She will meet a Supermouse.' Ma looked younger and more cheerful than I had ever seen her. 'Poor Old X-ray,' she said. 'Lots of tiny Supermice.'

'Old X-ray doesn't seem to worry about the time,' I said to test her.

'Nor do I. Race you to the house.' Ma ran, reaching the house before me, running like a young girl, which she was not.

That night, before getting into my four-poster, I wrote by the light of a candle to Mr Bailey.

> Dear Mr Bailey,
>
> We have reached Haphazard House. Please come. There is a toad. Your room is ready.
>
> Love,
>
> Lisa Fuller.

Mr Bailey, I felt, would understand; he of all people, whose job was to watch time passing on meters. I found an envelope and a stick of sealing wax. I melted it in the candle and, licking my thumb, pressed it on the hot blob. As I settled my head on the pillow I recollected that some meters went out of order, stopped, but I was too tired to care.

Chapter 16

I told Ma at breakfast that I had written to Mr Bailey.

'I'm glad. I must remember to pay him for that taxi.'

Pa gulped down the rest of his coffee. 'Come on, Miss Pin, I want to paint you, catch you while I can.'

'Sure.' Victoria resumed the American accent. 'Sure, anything you say. D'you want my glasses?'

'Yes, the elbows and the beads.' Pa measured her with his eyes.

'I'll take care of Baby.' Edward took Baby from Victoria.

'Don't lose sight of him, honey.'

'I won't.' Edward watched Victoria follow Pa. He carried Baby away on his shoulder. Grandpa, sitting with Old X-ray on his lap, watching Angelique treading delicately among the breakfast cups on the table, grunted. 'Our Coco, *now* he can paint.' He held Old X-ray's ears between finger and thumb, stroking them.

'Anyone want anything in the village?' I asked. 'I'm going to explore.'

David looked up from his book. 'See if there's a paper.'

'There won't be.' Grandpa went on caressing Old X-ray. She shut her eyes. Ma picked up Angelique, about to lick the butter, and put her on the floor.

'There won't be a paper,' said Grandpa.

'Why should there be no paper?' Ma leant close to Grandpa and kissed his cheek. 'You haven't shaved.'

'There's plenty of time for that.' He stroked Old X-ray's nose, pressing gently up from her pink nose to her forehead.

'Why no paper?' Ma's voice was low.

'Nobody to read it.'

'There's us.'

'You sure?'

'Of course I'm sure; well, pretty sure.'

Grandpa laughed. 'You're not sure, and who in the village wants a paper?'

'I don't know. I've only met Mr Pearce and his wife.'

'Guardians of village news.'

'It's funny we've only met *them*.'

Old X-ray climbed slowly down Grandpa's leg, letting her tail slide through his fingers.

'You said there was a school in the next village,' I said.

'Well, I suppose there is as there isn't one here.'

Grandpa looked at me from under wrinkled lids. 'Time for you to trot off,' he said. 'Enjoy yourself.'

'I shall,' I said, feeling brave, and set off to discover Coldharbour. I would post my letter and explore.

It had rained in the night and walking through the wood drops fell on my head. The air smelt of grass and leaves. Pigeons cooed, jays chattered, out of sight. In a clump of hazels long-tailed tits hunted in a flock. When I reached the road I saw the church tower, rearing like an Egyptian dog, ears pricked. Swallows dived and swooped round the pinnacles. The churchyard was crowded with headstones in long grass; tall stones, short stones, plain stones, stones decorated with curlicues; in the grass, poppies and columbines swayed. I read the inscriptions: died aged 96, died aged 70, died aged 6 months, 9 years, 4 months—there was no rule. The stones leaned north, south, east, west, bowing and tilting in a dance. A nice place to lie, I thought, and remembered my letter.

I pushed open the door of the post office. A bell fixed to the door made a horrible noise. Behind the counter a grey-haired woman observed me through fancy spectacle frames. I said, 'Good morning.'

She said, 'Good morning.' We paused, she sizing me up.

'Might I have a stamp, please?'

'A stamp.' She spoke emphatically. 'A stamp.'

'Yes, please.' I produced my letter.

'First class?' She reached for the letter and looked at it. 'First class for Mr Bailey of Islington, London.'

'Yes, please.' I was nettled.

'No need to be nettled. I am Mrs Pearce.' She opened a folder, extracted a stamp, licked it and placed it in the corner of my letter then gave it a thump. 'There.' She looked satisfied. 'You put it in the box. What's your name?'

'Lisa.'

'And your brother?'

'Josh.'

'Short for Joshua?'

'I suppose so.'

'You suppose?'

'Well, it is.'

'Then you should say so.'

I fidgeted from one foot to another, staring at Mrs Pearce.

'And your ma's a lovely lady and your pa paints pictures, the modern variety.'

'Yes.'

'Mr Hayco was given that way.'

'Old Mr Hayco who died? He painted?'

'Not exactly.'

'Not exactly dead or didn't exactly paint?' Two could play this game.

'Artistic.' Mrs Pearce was not giving in. 'A collector. And there's a young man called David who owns that van.'

'Yes.' I felt she wanted me to defend the van, those jolly nymphs and daisies, so I just said 'Yes'.

'And two young people with a child.'

'Yes.'

'They won't be staying.'

'Why won't they?' Mrs Pearce eyed me without deigning to answer. I decided to outstare her; take an inventory of Mrs Pearce as she was taking one of me. She had an upholstered front down which cascaded row on row of pink pearls. I began to count them.

'And you brought a dog.'

'And a cat and a kitten.' I was tired of saying 'Yes' like an idiot.

'That would be Rags.'

'His name is Bogus. He comes from the Battersea Dogs' Home. He was lost.'

'I should just think he was, poor Rags.' Mrs Pearce showed emotion, her eyes shining through the spectacle frames which were pink like the pearls. 'Poor, dear Rags.'

'His name is Bogus.'

'So you say.'

'Why won't Victoria and Edward stay?' I latched on to her remark like a dropped stitch.

'They can't, dear; not that lot.'

I had counted up to nine rows, hesitated and started again from the top of her chin.

'Mr Pearce thought Bogus was Rags, too.' I attacked boldly.

'Couldn't be, could he?' Mrs Pearce smiled mockingly. Her pearly teeth were almost pink. 'Disappeared after the fire.'

'That was in 1949,' I said.

'That's right, that was the year.'

'Were you here?'

'Oh yes, we are always here, George and I.'

'As postmistress and builder?'

'You can call us that if you like.'

'Oh.' We eyed one another. I didn't feel I was getting much information. I couldn't make out whether there were nine or ten rows of pearls on that vast bosom.

'There are ten, dear.' Mrs Pearce grinned. Then, putting out a plump hand, said, 'Another stamp?' in the tone people use when they offer another cake as though one had eaten too many already. 'And your pa has a hat.' She looked slyly at me. 'Perhaps you will like it here.' She folded her hands on the counter.

'We do,' I said, disliking her. 'What do people do here?' I would not discuss the hat.

'I run the post office and George has his business.'

'But other people?'

'There aren't other people, not often; they don't do anything as they aren't here.'

'There's us.' I spoke more bravely than I felt.

'Yes, there's you. Sure you won't have another stamp?'

'Quite sure, thank you. I must go now. Goodbye.'

'Goodbye,' said Mrs Pearce.

I paused by the door, curious. 'In what way was Mr Hayco artistic?'

'In various ways—a bit untimely.'

'Unsuitable, d'you mean?'

'My husband thought so about some things. They fell out.'

'Quarrelled?'

'What, dear?'

'You said Mr Hayco and your husband fell out. What about?'

'Did I, dear? I don't believe I did. We were talking about Rags. He *was* a nice dog—followed his master everywhere.'

'Dogs do,' I said coldly, angry that she would not tell me about her husband and Mr Hayco.

'And the baby is called Arnold. Isn't that nice.'

'It's an awful name,' I said.

'If you say so.' Mrs Pearce seemed to dismiss me. I opened the door and the bell clattered above my head. 'Thank you.'

'Goodbye and thank *you*,' Mrs Pearce called after me.

I sat on the churchyard wall. The village was very quiet. In villages in France people stood in groups talking, cats sunned themselves, dogs scratched their fleas; here there was no sign of life. I supposed everybody went off to work in the place Ma said we would go to school. The post office was the only shop. It seemed funny that I should be the only person to be seen. A sign outside a gate said, *George Pearce, Builder and Decorator*. Our Mini stood forlorn by the side of the road. I averted my gaze. It was stupid to be sentimental about bits of metal, but in her day Mini had been a car of character, especially when driven by Pa, as witnessed bumps and scratches on her bodywork. Poor Mini. I waved to her, kicking my heels on the wall.

Up the hill, walking slowly, came Grandpa and Josh. Bogus was with them, feathery tail aloft. I went to meet them.

'What news?' asked Grandpa.

'The village seems empty.'

'Then I shall fill the pub. I have a great thirst.' Grandpa stepped into the pub. Josh joined me on the wall and looked about him.

'Not much going on.'

'Nothing,' I said. 'Did you go into the post office yesterday?'

'Yes. Ma did her shopping there; it's run by Mrs Pearce.'

'I bought a stamp from her. She asked me a lot of questions.' Remembering my letter, I crossed the road and put it in the letterbox. As I rejoined Josh a bus lumbered up the hill and stopped. No one got in or out and it moved on out of sight.

'Coldharbour isn't exactly a hive of activity. Let's visit the church.' Josh kicked his heels against the wall and dropped beside me. We walked round the church and went in. 'What about Bogus?' Josh asked.

'Don't be boring,' I said. 'God made Bogus. He can come in.'

There was a beautiful screen and pulpit, and several nice tombs. 'Sacred to the memory of Hugh Hayco and his beloved wife Susanna who departed this life in the year of our Lord 1666.'

'They must have had the plague,' I said, staring at the prostrate figures carved in marble. 'I wonder whether he really loved her.'

'They couldn't put that they hated each other's guts. Look, a butterfly.' Josh pointed to a butterfly fluttering in a shaft of light. 'Let's get it out.'

We pulled some cords and opened a window. Josh moved away. I stood watching while the captive fluttered from one shaft of light to another, wishing it towards the open window. Bogus climbed into the pulpit and, standing on his hind legs, looked down on me, ears aflop. The butterfly flew out into the open air. I heaved a sigh of relief.

'Hey, Lisa, come here,' Josh called from the foot of the tower. 'Look at this.' He had found a door to the crypt.

'Look, coffins.' Josh ran ahead, examining large, small and medium coffins ranged round the walls.

'There's even one for an infant,' said Josh, 'quite posh handles.'

'They're rather horrible,' I said.

'I like them. D'you think this suits me?' Josh lay down in a coffin, closed his eyes and crossed his hands. Bogus climbed in on top of him.

'Stop fooling, Josh. It's not funny to be dead.'

'How d'you know? We may die and, oops, we'll hear the Last Trump and be at a party.'

'Don't invite *me*.' I backed away up the stairs.

'We are all invited,' Josh called after me. I ran out and was glad to see the pub door opening and Grandpa come out. His step was sprightly, he was laughing, throwing back his head. He looked a lot less bald than usual, his trousers less baggy.

'Grandpa—'

'Where's that boy?'

'In the crypt. He's lying in a coffin with Bogus, pretending to be dead.'

'Is he indeed, morbid boy.'

'There are a lot of coffins ready. Grandpa, get him out of there, please.' I pulled at his hand nervously.

'Nothing to worry about.' Grandpa raised his voice and shouted, 'Out, come out,' very loudly.

'I've never heard you shout so loudly,' I said in astonishment.

'Coldharbour air's cleared my pipes.' Josh and Bogus came out of the church. 'Don't make bad taste jokes, boy.'

'Sorry.' Josh looked at Grandpa. 'What's happened to you?'

'Had a good pint of beer.'

'You are taller,' said Josh.

'More hair, less wrinkles,' I said. 'There's something funny about this village.'

Grandpa started briskly down the hill towards Haphazard. 'He looks younger,' I said.

'Don't be absurd,' Josh crushed me. 'He's just feeling cheerful.'

I ran to catch up with Grandpa. 'Was the pub nice?'

'Yes. Landlord is that Pearce fellow. Made himself agreeable.'

'Anybody else in there?'

'No, just me. Had the place to myself.'

'Grandpa, there is nobody in the village except Mr Pearce and Mrs Pearce. Don't you think it strange? No cats, dogs, women or children. The bus stopped and no one got out. I didn't even see a driver.'

'You talk too much,' Grandpa snarled. I stopped in my tracks and waited for Josh.

'I heard.' Josh grinned at me. 'He was beastly.'

'Mr Pearce reminds me of someone we know and Mrs Pearce, too.'

'I know,' said Josh, breaking into a trot to keep up with Grandpa. 'The Lollipop lady and the Lollipop man in Croydon.'

'The ones Pa called Mr and Mrs Charon and said, "look it up in the dictionary"?'

Josh nodded. 'He had something to do with a ferry.'

Grandpa waited for us to catch up. He looked amiable again. 'It's time for lunch.'

'Mr Pearce and Mrs Pearce behave as if they knew Bogus,' I said.

'A long time ago,' Josh stressed, 'and they knew Baby.'

'All babies look alike. Like Chinese,' Grandpa mocked.

'No two Boguses would.' We all laughed at this.

'So if they knew Bogus in 1949 that time was the time that it is now—'

'I am content with time for lunch,' Grandpa stated, 'for today at least.'

We came out of the wood and looked across to the house waiting for us. From the window above the porch the person waved before retreating into shadow.

'Did you see?' Josh and I spoke together. 'Grandpa, did you see?'

'Yes, yes,' he said testily. 'Don't fuss.'

Ma came out of the house to meet us. Walking beside her was Mr Bailey, smiling broadly. 'Soon as I got your letter I came. No time like the present, I said. Time to be off, I said. I downed my book of parking tickets and here I am. What's the matter then?' He stared at me gaping. 'Don't want me after all then? Ain't there no toad?'

'Of course there is.' I grabbed his hand. 'Come, I'll show you.' I led him to the walled garden. How could I tell him I had only posted my letter half an hour before?

Chapter 17

'How did you get here, Mr Bailey?'

'Hitched a lift down the M4 to Bristol in a Jag. I knew the driver, booked him last winter. He didn't recognize me out of uniform. In Bristol I had some fish and chips. Then down the M5 in a Ford, a lorry to Coldharbour, then a bus dropped me by the village.'

'We saw the bus but we didn't see you.'

'Then I walks through the wood to the 'ouse and meets your ma. Where's the toad then?'

'This way.' I led him to the wall and pointed to the clump of iris. 'He went in there yesterday.'

'Couldn't have been yesterday. That's when I got your letter. You just try and be accurate. In my job you have to be accurate otherwise it's unfair. You keep a strict account of time, see?'

'Just try here!' I exclaimed. 'Time is absolutely haywire, Mr Bailey, it's gone mad.'

'How's that?' Mr Bailey squatted, peering down among the iris leaves. I told him about posting my letter, about Mr Pearce and Bogus, Grandpa's odd appearance coming out of the pub, Mrs Pearce's conversation; and while I was about it I told him about the person who watched and waved. Mr Bailey's eyes were on a level with the spiky leaves.

'They burrow,' he said. 'He may have burrowed. They hibernate, though it's early in the year yet.'

'Are you listening to what I'm telling you?' I was indignant that he seemed unmoved.

'Yes I am. Ah! There he is! See 'is eye? See it blink? He's the very colour of the roots, the clever chap.' Mr Bailey sat back on his heels, elated.

'Mr Bailey, I'm trying to tell you things about time. Are you deaf, or what?'

'I'm not deaf. If you'd heard as many versions of time as I have you would be unmoved. Unmoved,' he repeated, not taking his eyes off the toad. '"No time at all, Mr Warden,"' he mimicked a woman's voice. '"Just time to change my books at the library,"'—a man's voice. 'Oxbridge, that one, they're the worst. "Just time to collect my mail from the Club." Superior officer type, greatcoat and bowler 'at. "Time to slip into Fortnum's." "Time to trot into the Haymarket." Trot! I give 'im trot. They all talk about time as if they knew, but the blooming meter knows the time until she goes wrong and then nobody knows, so what's the fuss?'

'Aren't you surprised?'

'Not really, no.'

'And what about the person in the hat. We've all seen him.'

'Wot sort of 'at. Not a bowler?'

'No. A hat like Pa's.'

'Something funny about that 'at, ain't there?'

'Well, yes.'

'So this person wears it?'

'A hat like it—another hat.'

'Shouldn't worry. Ain't no law about looking out of windows; no meter, no time limit, no law about 'ats, either.'

'You got the letter I posted to you this morning, yesterday. Aren't you surprised, even a little? Don't you think ... ' I stopped. Mr Bailey was tickling the toad's back with a long grass.

'Likes that, don't 'e?' I could happily have hit him.

'You shouldn't monkey about with time.' He observed my rage.

'It's monkeying about with us.'

'Pity the dog can't talk.' Mr Bailey picked his teeth thoughtfully with the stiff end of the grass.

'So you believe me?'

'Oh, yes. We've got away from meters here so maybe it's more lax. Nothing to grumble at.' He prodded hard at a tooth. 'You got your teeth done blue; how are they?'

'It wore off,' I said haughtily, 'in no time.'

'No call to be snooty.' He leaned down again to poke the toad. 'Eh, look at that, 'e's got a mate.' Interested, in spite of myself, I looked and saw indeed that beside the toad was a smaller one.

'Marvellous camouflage those roots. Wonder how old they are. No bigger than your fingernail when they stops being tadpoles. Lose their tails like your 'umans coming out of nappies. They're beautiful,' Mr Bailey crooned.

'Grandpa's getting on but he looked years younger when he came out of the pub.'

'Is that so?'

'Yes, more hair, his trousers weren't so baggy, and less wrinkles. It was rather peculiar.'

''E's a peculiar old gent.'

'He's not!'

'Nicely so. Looks a bit like them toads. They all 'ave wrinkled necks. That's praise coming from me.'

I laughed. 'It's not normal to grow suddenly—well, younger.'

'I wonder what normal is.' Mr Bailey straightened up and turned towards the house. 'I'm hungry, that's normal. Now them toads, when they're hibernating they don't eat for months. That's normal for them. It's a matter of time between meals.'

'You don't seem to realize,'—I followed him along the path—'that time is hopping about like your toads.'

'Toads don't 'op, it's frogs that 'op.'

'I suppose so.' I was sulky.

'So there's time like toads and time like frogs and time like 'umans, and here it's got into a *mélange*. That's French for time for dinner.' Mr Bailey laughed. 'Or what happens to your dinner when you've ate it. *Mélange* is French for mix, see? That's a joke, you should laugh.'

'I don't think it's funny,' I said, feeling prickly fear set my fingers tingling, tightening my chest. 'I'm frightened,' I said. 'There's something very peculiar—'

'Nah!'

'Yes, there is.'

Mr Bailey looked at me curiously.

'To me, anyway.' I put my hand in his for safety. 'Also,' I said, feeling better, 'the female toad is larger than the male.'

'Believe you're right.' Mr Bailey's hand felt dry like the toad. 'Take a tip from me, young Lisa.' Mr Bailey held my hand firmly. 'When you're afraid you say to yourself, "I'll forget that". Repeat that after me.'

'I'll forget that,' I said, feeling comforted.

'That's right, you forget it.'

Chapter 18

The shriek we heard as we approached the house stopped us dead. It came clear and high from Pa's studio, a top note worthy of Maria Callas, such absolute terror that I felt my hair crackle. Shriek followed shriek. Ma and David rushed out of the house jostled by Grandpa. Victoria, long hair streaming, raced to the house, her skirts held high. She bounded into the house and began scrambling up the ladder. Halfway up she met Edward, carrying Baby, hurrying down. For a moment they swayed in a group, then the ladder slipped sideways and decanted them. We were picking them up and trying to see whether anyone was hurt when Pa arrived, breathless, holding a paintbrush.

'What did you do to her?' Ma stopped brushing Victoria down.

'Nothing,' said Pa furiously. 'I was painting the girl, told her she could rest. She took a look at the canvas and let out a yell. I must say I've put up with some harsh criticism in my life but never a model who had the vapours. Hah!' Pa was shaken. Victoria was clinging to Edward, clutching Baby, at the same time squeezing him so hard that he began to whimper and then to yell. She pointed a trembling finger at Pa. 'You, you, you were—' Her voice trailed. 'I, I was—'

Pa threw down the paintbrush and stamped his foot. 'I was doing very well, got those spiky elbows and goofy glasses. All I needed was your idiotic beads and skirts and I'd have got you. Hah!' He raised his fists in the air and stamped. He also cried 'Hah!' for the third time. There was a silence.

'Nobody hurt?' David gave the ladder a little shake.

'Coco is hurt.' Grandpa let out a guffaw. 'His artistic pride.'

'Grandpa.' Ma spoke very quietly. 'Will you please shut up?'

'Glad to oblige.' Grandpa made a bow and walked away.

'Come for a little walk.' Edward drew Victoria away, reaching his arm up to her waist. Victoria shook herself free.

'I'm sorry. I don't know what came over me. I've hurt your feelings.' She turned to Pa who still stood with his fists in the air.

'That's quite all right. Criticism's good for the soul—' Pa's face cleared.

'I was about to call you for lunch. I've something I want to say to you.' Ma asserted her authority. We followed her into the kitchen.

'Where is Josh?' Ma looked round.

'Here,' Josh appeared, out of breath. 'I heard shrieks so I came to see who's been murdered.'

'That'll do.' Ma quelled him. 'Will you all sit down.'

We sat round the table waiting for her to begin.

'Well now. I daresay some of you have noticed things which are out of the ordinary, but first I suggest that we need a staircase from the hall to the first floor. Either we buy one or make one. We don't want Baby who is young, or Grandpa, who is old, falling down, though people seem to be able to fall in a heap and come to no harm—' She was interrupted by laughter. 'So will you all be careful with the ladder until we get some stairs?'

'We could ask Mr Pearce,' Josh suggested.

'You can ask but he won't.' Pa stood up. 'I must get back to work.' He left the room.

'I'll sit for you tomorrow,' Victoria called after him.

'What upset my little pet?' Edward looked into her face protectively. Ma supressed a smile.

'I'd rather not say, not now.' Victoria was still tremulous.

'Then let's give Baby an airing.'

'Yes, let's do that.'

Ma sighed. 'Who is left to eat lunch?'

'I'm ravenous,' I said.

'Me too,' said Josh.

'I am in need of sustenance and so is Mr Bailey after his journey, and David.' Grandpa sat down at the table. 'Smells good.' He nodded towards the stove.

Ma brought food from the range, putting the dishes on the table.

'Help yourselves,' she said, sitting down beside Grandpa.

'Where did all this come from? We didn't bring it from the village.' David helped himself to beans and peas.

Ma smiled. 'That's one of the things I wanted to say. I found them in the scullery this morning: beans, peas, tomatoes and strings of onions hung on the beams, and garlic.'

'Who brought them in?'

'Your guess is as good as mine,' said Ma. 'Lisa has heard someone at work but we haven't seen him.'

'The fellow who waves?' Grandpa spoke as though to be

waved to from above the porch was the most normal thing in the world.

'Anybody seen him clearly?' David spoke with his mouth full.

'You are unlikely to see him clearly,' said Grandpa. 'Some may not see him at all.'

'You sound as though you knew him,' I said.

'Better than most of you, if he is who I believe he is.'

'I wonder what he means by that.' Josh spoke low. 'Ask him.'

'I don't like to.' We ate our meal in silence.

Looking at Ma, sitting with the sun shining on her, I was puzzled. She sat relaxed and easy. In Croydon she had been tense and drawn. Now her hair showed no grey and her face was smoother than I had ever seen it. She and Grandpa had shed years. I looked at David and Josh. Neither was in any way different. Nor was Mr Bailey.

'Who brings in the veg then?' Mr Bailey asked suddenly. 'Fairies?'

Ma got up and began to gather plates. 'Put these in the scullery.' She handed a pile to Josh who took them out.

'Ma,' Josh called. The plates clattered as he put them down.

'What is it?'

'Masses of strawberries, Ma, but masses!' Josh came back carrying a basin full of fruit.

'Well, I would like to thank whoever it was,' Ma exclaimed. 'I heard nothing. Did any of you?' We shook our heads. 'Not a sound,' said Josh.

'Somebody must be pleased to have us here,' said Ma. 'The furniture is arranged for us, wonderful stuff brought in from the garden, the ash in the fireplace warm. I am so grateful, so happy.'

Pa came in. 'Any lunch left? Inspiration has left me. That girl's shrieks drove it away.'

'Not for ever, I hope.' Ma got up to get Pa food.

'One can never feel safe,' said Pa soberly, accepting a plate. 'Have you all finished?'

'No.'

'Good.' Pa ate in silence for a while. 'Did those two leave for the afternoon? If she'd come back I could recapture her.'

'She didn't like what she saw,' said Ma. 'What did you do to frighten her?'

Pa was morose, pushing away his plate. 'I was working; it was going well. I told her to rest; she looked at what I'd done and let out those yells.' He looked up. 'Hush. Here they come.'

Victoria and Edward could be heard talking as they came in. 'Lunch?' said Ma quickly.

'Thanks—if we aren't too late.' Victoria, calm now, sat down with Baby on her knee, Edward beside her. Ma and Josh dished out food. Pa looked at Victoria surreptitiously. Victoria, aware of this, pretended not to notice. A small awkward silence grew into a larger one.

'We miss the telly.' Edward spoke, suddenly aggressive. 'We miss electricity.'

'Victoria gave out some pretty electric yells.' Grandpa chuckled evilly.

'Oh, please.' Ma put her hand on Grandpa's. 'Do resist.'

'I find the candlelight beautiful.' David, not given to voicing an opinion, did so now. Edward and Victoria looked at each of us in a worried way.

'Why don't you go to the pub?' asked Ma gently.

'Bad for Baby.' Victoria's arm tightened slightly round Baby's waist so that he turned and looked up into her face.

'I'll mind Baby if you leave him with me,' Ma offered.

'Thank you, but we'd rather not. It's better not to leave him. He wouldn't be safe.' Ma raised her eyebrows.

'Come on.' Edward spoke roughly. 'We must hurry if we're to catch the bus.' He jerked Victoria to her feet.

'They had hardly any lunch.' Ma watched them go.

'That's how she gets those elbows.' Pa helped himself to strawberries. 'Doesn't eat enough.'

'You'd think they were afraid of losing him.' Ma was amused. 'They think he might get stolen.'

'Stolen!' I exclaimed. 'Babies only get stolen by frustrated girls outside supermarkets. Who'd want to steal Baby?'

'They are catching a bus to see a supermarket. That will make them feel safer.' David got up and left the room, followed by Josh.

'They will wander along the High Street and look at the shops. They will find a television shop and watch colour TV through the glass. They will be reassured. Come on, Father, let's have a go at you.' Pa and Grandpa went off, leaving me with Ma.

'You started off about the stairs,' I said as I wiped the plates.

'I did.'

'Why didn't you go on then?'

'I don't know. There's some mystery. Remember Mr Pearce's reaction that first morning?'

'That first morning it was—' I paused, wondering when that first morning had been. 'How long have we been here?' I looked at Ma.

'I don't know,' she said. 'Ten days? Weeks? Does it matter? I don't think it matters much.' I watched her go back to the kitchen. She began collecting the copper pots and pans so that, afraid of being asked to help clean them, I left her. 'There will come a time when you stop being allergic to Brasso,' she called after me.

In the walled garden Mr Bailey sat by the well contemplating the clump of irises. 'Hello,' I said.

'Sit down and be quiet.'

I sat down beside him, waiting for the toads.

'Night-time's the time they move around,' he said. 'In summertime.'

'You sure they know the time?'

Mr Bailey did not deign to answer.

I watched Old X-ray strolling along the top of the garden wall, followed by Angelique. 'She's grown,' I said.

'Who?'

'Angelique. She was born the day we met you. Look at her now.'

'Looks full grown.' Mr Bailey glanced up at the cats then back at the toads' hideout.

'Angelique's only a few weeks old,' I said. 'She was born on Derby Day, don't you remember?'

'Quite a time you had that day. Bought an 'at, backed an 'orse, won a fortune, 'ad your teeth painted, but you're right, that cat ain't 'ad time to grow so big.'

I looked at Angelique, beautiful and shining, nearly as elegant as Old X-ray and just as large.

'You call her "Old X-ray" but she don't look old.' He watched Old X-ray suddenly rush along the wall, followed by Angelique. 'There now, they've gone. Here one minute, gone the next, like my aitches. Have you noticed I drop them?'

'Sometimes.'

'My old ma wore stays and sometimes when she was tired she'd loosen them, made 'er feel easy, see, Now I do the same with my aitches; verbal instead of physical. When I'm tired, see. I'm tired now. I'm off to 'ave a nap.'

'It's all that time you spent on the road; such a long time, Mr Bailey.'

'Enough of that. It's too dodgy. You leave time alone.' He nodded towards the clump of irises. I peered down at the toads and wondered how much time must pass before one of them moved. The sun was hot on my back, the garden very quiet.

Chapter 19

I bent over the iris leaves and studied the toads. The larger toad blinked. I picked it up. I liked the feel of its skin, cool and dry. She sat on my hand, sides pulsing, body stout below her shoulders, legs folded on either side of her narrow waist. I held her against my cheek. 'Like a swim?' On impulse I leaned over the side of the well and let her plop into the dark water. Shocked, she began to swim. I was filled with remorse. There was no toehold on the smooth side. She scrabbled futilely. Her neck looked dreadfully like Grandpa's.

I ran to the toolshed, snatched a hoe and, running back, held it down to the toad. 'Climb up,' I whispered, afraid of somebody discovering my cruelty, afraid of frightening the toad still more. The toad swam away from the hoe then rested, its legs sinking in the water.

I swung my legs over the side and let myself down into the water. The cold made me gasp; my feet touched slippery bottom, then slid and my head went under. As I came up the toad was level with my nose. I put my hand under its stomach and she rested quietly, drawing in her legs. The water reached to my armpits. I stretched up with my free hand. The top of the wall was out of reach. I attempted to jump, my feet slid again and I lost the toad who swam, scrabbling at the sides. I put my hand under it again. I stood in the dark water and wondered how much time before I drowned. 'Not much time,' I said to the toad. She blinked. I put my free hand over her, and held her caged lightly between my fingers. She felt warmer than the water. I drew a deep breath and shouted 'Help! Help! Help!' My voice sounded odd, bouncing off the side of the well.

'Help!' I roared. The air was very still. The insects hummed loudly, and the sound of a bird's wings as it flew across the garden was clear, the displacement of air with each flap of wings distinct. I wondered where everyone could be. How long since Mr Bailey had left me? I would be missed at the next meal. How much time did it take to die of exposure? 'Help!' I cried, pitching my voice high so that it would carry like Victoria's. My cry sounded pitifully weak compared with hers. 'Help!' I tried again and listened.

I heard the tinkle of metal on stone, a scratching in the earth, a cough. The invisible gardener was working, his hoe scraping through the earth. He cleared his throat, whistled. I was so terrified I let out a yell which beat Victoria's. The toad stirred uncomfortably between my hands.

When I heard someone above me I hardly dared look. Bogus was hanging his head over the parapet.

'Oh, Bogus.' I began to cry, sobbing and hiccuping. Bogus became excited and barked into the well, whining, trying to reach me. 'Careful, careful!' I screamed. 'You'll fall in.' He lost his balance, fell in with an almighty splash, thrashing the water, scratching my chest with his paws, out of his depth. He will drown, I thought, and so will I.

'If only you were the Frog Prince,' I said to the toad, letting it go so that I could hold Bogus. The toad attached herself to Bogus's neck and, supported by me, he stopped panicking. I wondered how long it would be before Bogus became waterlogged.

A shadow obscured the light. Above us on the parapet a ginger cat sat looking down, his tail lashing from side to side. Bogus made a throttling, whining noise which in any other circumstances would have meant pleasure. The cat looked down with large, green eyes. Striped like a tiger, it opened its mouth and yowled a long echoing yowl, arched its back, the sun glinting on its stripes. Time for another shriek I thought and, closing my eyes, opened my mouth and screamed.

Suddenly Bogus was lifted up from the water. The water streamed off him into my eyes and the toad fell into my hands. Half blinded by the water, I looked up. Hands reached down, caught me under the armpits. I was lifted clear and put down, holding the toad guiltily in one hand, trying to wipe the water away from my eyes with the other. For a moment I saw a man, nearly as tall as Pa. He stooped to pat Bogus. I tried to see his face but it was hidden by the brim of a Panama hat. He was there, then he was gone.

The ginger cat vanished. The garden was empty except for me and Bogus, and the toad—uncomfortably squeezed in my hand making an orange mess. Trembling, I put her back in the clump of iris.

'It was Pa,' I said to Bogus who was rolling against a clump of catmint. But I knew it was not Pa as I tried to squeeze the water from my clothes.

I waited to experience terror. I expected extreme terror. I felt I should be in a state of terror, the natural thing to feel after being lifted from a well by someone who wasn't there. I felt no terror at all.

'Goodness, Bogus,' I said to him. 'I am not in a state of terror.'

Then I was afraid. My voice was not my voice, not the voice of a child but a deeper, older voice, almost the voice of a woman.

I ran.

I ran to Pa's loft. I had to see him. I raced up the steps leading to Pa's loft and pushed open the door. Pa looked up in irritation; it was unheard of to interrupt him at work.

'What is it?' He sounded ungracious. 'Why d'you interrupt me?'

'Pa... I... Pa, I fell into the well, Pa. I was fished out. Bogus fell in, too. I can't explain. There was a ginger cat, and a—a—man in a hat. Oh, Pa—'

Pa sighed. He had been painting Grandpa. He covered the canvas with a cloth.

'All right, Father, it's gone. Another day perhaps.' Pa's expression was strange as though he were elsewhere, not looking at me—dripping wet after nearly drowning. I looked from Pa to Grandpa and the covered canvas. Did Pa see Grandpa as I did now—a man of about fifty with a thatch of grey hair, elegant nose, beetling eyebrows, alert eyes?

Grandpa took my hand. 'Lisa, you are soaked.'

'Grandpa, you looked—'

'I know, I know, that's how I was feeling.'

'So much younger,' I blurted out. 'Hardly older than Pa.'

'Nothing to worry about.' The hand which gripped mine was the gnarled hand I knew, wrinkled with brown marks and swollen joints; his face looking at me old, leathery, not unlike the toad's. 'How did you get so wet?'

As we walked to the house I told him about the toad, the well, and Bogus falling in when I had shouted for help. I could not tell him about how I had been lifted out or by whom.

'There was a huge ginger cat.'

'A stray perhaps.'

'It didn't look like a stray, it looked—er—prosperous.'

'Some cats are. Old X-ray has recently grown prosperous. You say the bottom of the well was slippery,'

'Yes, like ice. I went under twice. I thought I was going to die.'

Grandpa laughed. 'You won't come to that that way.' He began to wheeze and stood to catch his breath. When we walked on a thought struck me.

'Grandpa, you've never let Pa paint you before have you? What made you change your mind?'

'This and that. Listen. Something's going on in the house. Listen to that racket.'

'It's Victoria again. I thought they'd gone to catch the bus.'

'Came back, said there was no bus, seemed to think there never would be a bus, said the postmistress says there never is a bus—'

'There is. I've seen it.'

'Well, they didn't. They jabbered about getting a fright in the churchyard? What were they doing in the churchyard?'

'It's very pretty.'

Grandpa laughed. 'So pretty they came running back, running all the way. Must have jogged that baby, churned up the child's dinner. Your mother smoothed them down, you know her clever way with ruffled feelings.' Grandpa wheezed again. 'Then she sent them up the ladder to rest. Wish I could get up the ladder—'

'But you can!'

'Don't trust it. Only been halfway. Haven't you noticed?'

'If you wanted to you could.'

'I sleep downstairs on the sofa. I'm waiting for the stairs; then I'll go up.'

'When you came out of the pub, and when Pa was painting you just now, you looked young enough to climb Everest.'

'Ah, but it doesn't always last.'

'So it's true you do get younger?'

'What's true varies. Come on, let's see what the hubbub is about.'

In the kitchen Victoria was screaming and shouting while Edward tried to calm her. David, Josh, and Mr Bailey stood around bawling excited questions. Ma stood watching. Baby bellowed, his face purple with the effort. Grandpa scrambled on to a chair with such alacrity I decided the ladder was a case not of 'can't' but 'won't'. He shouted above the din.

'What—is—going—on?'

Everyone stopped and stared up at Grandpa, agape. 'Well?'

'My beads.' Victoria was hysterical. 'My bean beads. They are gone—stolen.' She wrung her hands histrionically. 'They've gone—my beads, my beans.'

'Did you put them in the stew, my dear?' From the chair Grandpa looked down his beaky nose at Ma, his eyes flashing.

'That kind of remark is no help at all,' said Ma.

'Where did you see them last?' Josh was able to make himself heard.

'I wore them yesterday. They were by the bed this morning.'

'They'll turn up.' David, bored, turned and left the room.

'I know they won't.' Victoria weeping was beautiful.

'Sure they are not in the stew?' Grandpa stepped down gingerly from his chair, his hand on Josh's shoulder.

'Grandpa!' Ma spoke between clenched teeth.

'I was only trying to help.' Grandpa and Ma eyed one another.

'You can get other beans—' Josh suggested.

'No. Mine came from Brazil. We must go back.'

'Back to Brazil,' Josh was staggered.

'It's a "façon de parler'", said Mr Bailey. 'French for "push off 'ome".'

'Perhaps some clever dick's planted them.' Grandpa was laughing across the room at Ma.

'Don't—make—matters—worse,' she hissed at him.

A thought struck me. I left them and ran to the garden. In the stillness I listened, then I moved slowly, looking about me. Some earth was freshly tilled. I poked a finger into the earth and uncovered a pink bean. I squatted, looking down at the earth. 'All right,' I whispered to the still air. 'You know what you are doing.' I pushed the earth back over the bean and stood up. 'I shall forget you frightened me,' I said to the quiet air.

Later, Victoria and Edward left. Victoria carried Baby who waved goodbye with a fat little hand. Edward reached up to encircle Victoria's waist and hurried with short steps to keep up with her. 'It was bound to happen,' said Ma.

'I am sad,' I said. 'It is like a death.'

'A little.' Grandpa picked up Old X-ray and held her against his face. She looked away from him, twitching her tail.

'They left the van in the yard,' said Josh.

'They won't need it.' Old X-ray disengaged herself and dropped to the ground.

'Won't they come back?' I watched Victoria's skirt swishing into the wood.

'No, but your father caught her on canvas.'

'Oh, did he? In spite of the fuss?'

'Yes, wearing the hat.'

'The Panama,'

'He intends painting us all wearing that hat. "Hat Period" like Picasso's "Blue". The arrogance! I can still see them.' Grandpa peered across to the wood, his knobbly fingers shading his eyes.

'Oh.' Ma sounded distressed. 'Oh dear.'

Pa, who had been in the hall, joined us. 'What is it?' he said.

'They are stuck,' I said.

'Don't be ridiculous. Stuck? It's a trick of the light.'

I was right. Victoria and Edward were moving, but not into the wood or back to us. 'Go fetch them, Bogus.' Josh spoke low. 'Go fetch them.'

Bogus raced across the grass. We watched him bound through the slanting light to Edward and Victoria, jumping up and down, barking. But he jumped and bounded through them as though through a patch of mist. Mr Bailey, standing beside Grandpa, put his fingers to his mouth and whistled shrilly. Bogus hesitated, then came slowly back to us, his tail low, wagging apologetically.

'You don't want to lose the dog, do you?' Mr Bailey, watching Bogus, spoke harshly. I shivered.

'Come in all of you.' Ma was brisk. 'Lisa, you are wet. Go and change. Josh, go with her and see she puts on warm clothes. Andrew—' She looked at Pa. I thought she was crying. Pa put an arm round her and drew her into the house.

Josh followed me up the ladder. 'Time you and I had a talk,' he said as we reached my room. 'Nobody else seems to want to.'

I pulled my shirt over my head. 'The tricks aren't all tricks of light. There's something strange going on.'

Josh sat on the side of the bed pulling his knees up to his chin. 'It's haphazard. You must have noticed it comes and goes, without any logical reason.' Josh handed me a towel to dry my hair. 'What have you noticed?'

'Promise not to laugh.'

'I promise,' he said gravely.

I began. 'There's an invisible gardener. I can hear him working, but I can't see him.' I paused. For a moment I wondered whether I could tell Josh about being lifted out of the well by a man wearing a hat who vanished. I decided not to. Josh might scoff. Whatever happened with whoever, it was my affair. 'He brings Ma vegetables.'

'Go on.'

'Grandpa from time to time looks as young as Pa.'

'I've noticed that, too, and Ma has changed.'

'Somebody waves from the window. I can't find the room.'

'I've looked, too. He wears the hat, or one like it.'

'There's something very odd about the village. The only people in it are Mr Pearce and Mrs Pearce.'

Josh frowned. 'There are other people but they don't talk. They wave or nod as they pass. They seem a little surprised to see me.'

'What sort of people?'

'Ordinary. There are people, at least I think there are. There's the bus driver. They don't speak. I *think* I've seen them.'

'Have you noticed something peculiar has happened with time? It feels as if we'd been here months and not days.'

'Yes. Angelique has grown up and Old X-ray is much younger. She was pretty ancient in London.'

'And Bogus. The Pearces call him Rags and behave as though he'd been here when Mr Hayco died in 1949. It's just possible Bogus might be another dog who looks exactly like Rags. It's possible that we only have vivid imaginations.'

Josh moved to the window and leaned out while I pulled on jeans. 'There's one thing I haven't imagined,' he said.

'And what's that?'

'There's a child's grave in the churchyard, no date on it. The child was called Arnold.'

'There are lots of Arnolds besides Baby.'

'It's a fresh grave, no proper stone.'

'Doesn't mean a thing.' I spoke more robustly than I felt. 'If we start imagining Baby's not alive which he *is*, we'll start thinking there's a staircase to be found.'

'I believe there is, and a person waving.'

'Oh Josh, just because that house agent said the house is haunted—'

'You've heard the gardener, seen the man waving—look at that.' Josh pointed out of the window. 'Something going on there.'

'Just mist rising.' I leaned beside him. 'It's awfully pretty.'

The mist was delicate as a Shetland shawl eddying in the evening air between the house and the wood, spiralling anticlockwise.

'Look.' Josh gripped my arm. 'See that?' The mist parted for a moment to show figures waving, then thickened. We could see arms reaching up, beckoning.

'It's Edward and Victoria. They need help.' Josh rushed to the door. 'Quick.'

We scrambled down the ladder to the hall. Bogus was standing at its foot. He barred our way so that Josh nearly fell over him.

'Out of the way, Bogus, out of the way.' Josh was impatient.

'He wants us to take the hat.' I snatched the Panama from the hatstand and crammed it on my head. Josh pulled open the front door and we ran out into thick mist.

Holding hands, a thing we had not done for years, we ran towards the wood, Bogus close on our heels. The mist deadened sound.

'We are coming,' Josh called. 'Where are you?'

'Here.' Edward's voice was anxious. We saw them standing close together, Victoria's head above the mist, she tall and spindly beside short Edward. She held Baby high on her shoulder. Edward had his arm round her. 'What's going on?' I tried to be reasonable, tried to be calm.

'We are trying to get away. We are stuck here, it's crazy.' Edward was furious, afraid.

'I can't see, my glasses are misted.' Victoria was close to tears.

'Wipe them.'

'I daren't let go of Edward and Baby.'

'Here then, keep still.' I took the glasses off her nose and dried them. 'You don't need them anyway. They are only a joke—you said so.' I replaced the glasses.

'I've needed them here, I really have. That's one of the frightening things. But you wouldn't understand.'

'Try us,' I said. 'What d'you mean, you are stuck?'

'We can't get through the wood. It's been getting more difficult every day.' Victoria sounded childish.

'Don't be so infantile,' Josh scoffed.

'We knew you'd never believe us if we told you. We are infantile, that's just it.' Edward spoke with extreme exasperation.

'Tell,' I said.

'We wake in the night and find we are children,' Victoria whispered. 'The first time it happened we didn't know each other.' Victoria's eyes were enormous behind the pebble glasses. 'Edward had spots.'

'And no beard.' I was beginning to understand.

'He wouldn't have a beard as a child.' Josh burst out laughing.

'It's no laughing matter,' said Edward angrily.

I joined Josh in laughter.

'Don't you realize, you idiots,' cried Edward, 'we wake up as children *and Baby isn't there*.'

'Oh,' we said, aghast. 'Oh.' Then with more understanding, 'You go back to before he was born?'

'Yes.' Tears were pouring down Victoria's cheeks.

'Come *on*.' Josh spoke roughly. 'Come *on*. We'll get you away.' He snatched the hat from my head and put it on Victoria's. 'Hold on to each other and to us. Let's go.'

We hurried them through the wood. Nobody spoke until we reached the road.

'Did Pa paint you successfully?'

'*He* thought it a success.'

'You didn't?'

'I looked about six years old; it was gruesome. I had braces on my teeth and I wore glasses all the time then. One doesn't like to be reminded.'

'You are very beautiful now.' Edward looked up at her.

'You didn't think so the first time we woke up like that. You said—'

'Never mind what I said. I was upset, that's all. Unnerved.'

'All right.' Victoria was grudging. 'What do you think I felt?'

'We shall be at the bus-stop in a minute.' Josh was tactful.

'There isn't a bus.'

'Oh yes there is. We'll put you on it, see you safely off.'

'Really?'

'Yes, we promise.'

'You are going without your van,' I said tactlessly.

'You keep it,' Edward said kindly. 'It's had its day. You may find some use for the brass figures, but the engine's gone. I tried it and it's kaput. We thought we could escape in it but not since—' He stopped.

'Not since what?'

'We saw something horrid in the churchyard.'

'Oh that,' exclaimed Josh. 'No need to worry about that. I've seen it, too. It's nothing to worry about at all.'

'The figures are super, thanks a lot,' I said.

We reached the bus-stop. Edward and Victoria looked relieved.

'I can hear the bus.' Josh turned his head and we all heard the sound of an engine. 'Thanks for the loan.' Victoria took off the hat and gave it to Josh. 'And you can keep these as a memento.' She handed me the glasses. 'I won't need them any more.'

Baby blew a bubble from wet lips. The spit ran down his chin.

'My baby.' Victoria kissed him, giving him a squeeze. Josh averted his eyes.

The bus drew to a halt. People looked down at us in silence.

'Climb aboard,' cried Josh. Victoria bent and kissed us. Edward clasped our hands. 'Goodbye,' they said. 'Thanks a lot. We'll be all right now. Goodbye.'

They climbed into the bus, Victoria's long skirts swinging out in the mist; Edward, thick-set, his arm ready to put round her waist when they found a seat. We watched them sit down. Baby pressed his face to the window, licking the glass, smearing it. The bus moved off. We waved. From behind the steamy, spat-on glass they waved back.

'That's a relief.' I patted Bogus as we watched the bus disappear round a bend. 'I feel happy.'

'Me, too.' Josh glanced at me. 'It's fine for Grandpa. It would have been rather nice to have them to play with if you think of it.'

'They were afraid of losing Baby.'

'Wouldn't have frightened me. Did you see him lick the window? Smothered it with spit. Ugh!'

'*They* love him.' I laughed.

'Let's take a peep in the churchyard.' Josh put on the hat and we climbed into the churchyard.

'Where is the grave?'

'I'll show you.' The pollen from the grass stuck to his jeans. There was no sound except of rooks cawing. 'It's here.' Josh rounded a corner by the tower.

'Where?'

'It's gone. How extraordinary.'

'Are you sure it was here?'

'Of course. A small grave, fresh earth and a black wooden marker which had "Arnold" in white paint. I swear it was here.'

'I believe you,' I said soberly. 'It looks as though we saved his life.'

'The hat did.'

'Okay, the hat.' Josh touched it.

'Baby Arnold's time had gone a bit wonky.'

'And Victoria and Edward's. They were not like us. This was a holiday for them, not real as it is for us.'

Our parents and David were sitting on the terrace watching the moon rise. 'They all look pretty normal,' I said. 'They don't look as though anything out of the ordinary ever happened, or even if they'd notice if it did. It's like a sneezing fit. The world seems about to burst, then it's normal again.'

'Tell you what isn't ordinary,' said Josh, looking up behind the house. 'I've been up that hill to look down on Haphazard and the house isn't there. No house, no garden, just a meadow with sheep cropping the grass.'

'Goodness, what did you do?'

'Ran home helter-skelter, and the house was here and he was waving from the window.'

'Perhaps you'd better wear the hat another time.'

'Perhaps I had. Look, he's waving.'

We waved back to whoever he was and ran across the grass to our parents.

Chapter 20

'Have they gone?' Pa looked over the rim of his glass, sitting with his back to the house, long legs stretched out.

'Yes. Caught the bus.'

Pa looked thoughtful. 'I never really caught Miss Pin, try as I would. She sat for me and, blimey, what came on to the canvas was a plain child in pebble glasses with her teeth in braces.' He sipped his drink and sighed. 'Not the prettiest of sitters.'

'Didn't you try her in the hat?' Ma asked mildly.

'I thought of it too late. By then she'd seen my painting, taken offence and wouldn't pose any more. I shall have to rake my memory to get those sharp elbows, lanky hair, the swing of the skirts.'

'You should have tried the hat.' Ma had taken it from Josh and held it gently in her lap. 'If you'd worn it—'

'Could have worn his false nose.' Grandpa tossed the sentence over his shoulder.

'Grandpa, please,' Ma murmured. 'Just when we are so peaceful.'

'Checkmate.' Mr Bailey moved his bishop.

'I think you cheated but I'll let it pass.' Grandpa set the men up again. 'Do best to get on with your portrait of me,' he said. 'I shan't be around for ever.'

'For a long time yet,' I said, 'the way you carry on.'

'Don't be impertinent,' snapped Grandpa, moving his queen's pawn. 'One is always conscious of death, and the view from the bathroom window is no help.'

'What do you mean?' Mr Bailey was anxious to join whatever conversation there might be.

'The window looks down on the yard. There's a hearse—disguised—but champing to be off.' Grandpa removed his false teeth and snapped them like a castanet. Mr Bailey recoiled. Grandpa replaced the teeth. 'Your move,' he said.

Mr Bailey made a move.

'They gave us the van as a parting present,' said Josh casually. 'Those figures will be useful somewhere. They don't really look serious enough for a hearse.'

'Who wants to be serious?' Grandpa moved a pawn. 'I rode down in it. The cats liked it. Be different in a coffin, I daresay.'

'You wouldn't know much about it in your coffin.' Mr Bailey moved his knight. 'I once put a ticket on a hearse. Irish people—having a wake.'

'If you put that hat on my coffin like a fieldmarshal's whatsit I might resurrect.'

'I don't find this conversation edifying.' Ma grinned at Pa. 'I'm going to get supper. How those two ate, just like children, and the baby hardly at all.' She went into the house. I followed.

'Baby didn't eat much because he wasn't here much,' I said, hoping to surprise her.

'I know, love,' she said, 'none of them was.'

'Did you like Baby?'

'Well—'

'Josh and I didn't. He dribbled.'

'Babies do.' Ma was noncommittal. 'He was teething.'

'I wonder whether Mr Bailey will catch it,' I said, collecting knives and forks from a dresser.

'I doubt it.' Ma cut some onions from the string. 'Oh, look what's come in.' She sounded delighted.

The table in the scullery was loaded with spinach, new potatoes and raspberries. 'All grown with love,' she said.

'I wonder whether he planted the beans with love,' I muttered.

'The what, darling?'

'Nothing,' I said, glad to see Ma so happy.

Chapter 21

In my four-poster, Bogus at my feet, I lay thinking of Edward and Victoria. If they had stayed on we could have played together, presuming that they would have been the same age as us. Josh and I had never had many friends. I wondered what Edward, aged fourteen, would have been like. I tried, vainly, to imagine him without the beard. Victoria with pebble glasses and braces on her teeth was difficult, too. I kicked restlessly; Bogus grunted. I sat up, stretching out my hand to stroke his head. My room was lit by the moon. Idly I watched my hand stroking the silky ears. Puzzled, I looked at it; it was larger than usual. Startled, I felt my arms and my shoulders, kicked my feet about. My legs were longer than normal. I got out of bed and looked in the mirror. The girl in the glass was not me. I lifted my eyes to my face, pushing back my hair. I confronted her. She looked back at me with startled eyes. I wondered who she could be and waved. She waved.

'Bogus,' I called. My voice sounded different.

Bogus got off the bed and came to me, looking up, wagging his plumy tail. In the mirror he stood beside the girl, looking up at her. We stood confronting ourselves. I felt my hair, my face, my body. I could see the reflection in the mirror doing the same. Bogus sat down and started scratching. In the mirror he scratched, too. I heard my name called, 'Lisa? Lisa?' I had heard that voice before.

I stared at my reflection. I could not answer though I wanted to. Somewhere in the house was music. My feet began to tap. In a moment I was dancing. I danced; so did the reflection. A voice called, 'Lisa!' insistently.

The music stopped. I hurled myself into bed, dragging Bogus with me, pulling up the sheet, clutching Bogus. It was morning and my mother called, 'Lisa. Time to get up.' I dressed, scrambled down the ladder to the hall and ran to the kitchen. The woman standing by the stove was an older version of the girl in the mirror.

'What is it?' Ma smiled.

'A dream,' I said. 'I dreamed of music and that someone called me.'

'I called you,' said Ma.

'I thought it was a man's voice. I've heard it before.'

Ma said nothing, putting bacon on a plate, handing it to me. 'Eat it before it gets cold,' she said.

'Do you dream?' I asked her.

'I don't need to.' She sat opposite me across the table. 'Probably because I'm very happy here.'

'Oh Ma, were you not happy before? You had Pa, you had us.'

'Yes, but your Pa was not happy, nor were you children and your Grandpa was only kept alive by—'

'By what?'

'Cussedness, I suppose.' Ma grinned. She looked very like the girl in the mirror. I decided not to tell her, it might spoil her happiness. 'What keeps Grandpa alive now?' I asked.

'He's looking forward to something.'

'What on earth has he to look forward to at his age?' I exclaimed.

'Age is relative,' said Ma. 'The air here suits him as it did not suit Victoria and Edward.'

We heard Josh calling, 'Ma, Ma, look who has come to see us!' Walking towards the house came Josh with Sandy.

'Sandy!' Ma and I ran to meet them. 'Sandy, what brings you here? How nice to see you.' She sounded insincere.

'Business.' Sandy bent to peck Ma's cheek. 'You look pretty fit.'

'You are in time for breakfast. Come in.' I looked up. The person at the window, wearing the hat, waved mockingly. I waved back.

'I would have been here sooner,' Sandy was saying, 'but I had trouble with my car. As I was coming into your village I swerved to avoid a cat and the car stalled. Couldn't get it started again; had to leave it and walk. Luckily I ran into Josh.'

'Was it a ginger cat?' I asked.

'Yes. Huge brute, size of a tiger. D'you know it?'

'Sort of.'

'Couldn't find a soul to help me. There must be a garage.'

'There isn't,' said Josh.

'No *garage*? You *are* in the sticks.'

'No. Mini died.'

'Who was Minnie? Did she run a garage? Funny job for a woman.'

'Mini, our car.'

'That clapped-out old sardine tin? No garage could repair that.'

'She died in the village. Perhaps your car's dead, too,' Josh teased.

'Can't compare my Jaguar with your thing.'

Josh took offence. 'The village doesn't like cars.'

'He's only just arrived.' Ma hastened to make peace. 'It's great to see you Sandy, why have you come?'

'Andrew never answered my letters. I've written five.'

'I don't think he's had them, has he children?'

'No letters,' we chorused.

'That's absurd. I put the right address—Haphazard House, Coldharbour. It isn't an address you can get wrong, is it?'

'No,' we said. 'Not very easily.'

'I expect he destroyed them,' said Sandy querulously.

'He didn't get them,' said Ma. 'Tell us why you're here.'

'Time Andrew had another show. The public's crying out for another Andrew Fuller show.'

'But he's only just had one,' I said, 'in June, Derby Day. You must remember *that*.'

'That was years ago. He must have done some work since then.'

'Years?' I asked, puzzled.

'Yes, yes.' I caught Ma's eye. 'He's had plenty of time to paint enough for another show.'

'Ah, time,' said Ma, leading Sandy through the hall. 'Time to get you something to eat. You must be tired after your drive. Try and find your father, children.'

'I'll look in the loft,' said Josh.

'I'll look in the garden.'

'He won't be there.'

'He might be.'

In the garden Pa was sitting on the side of the well sketching.

'Hullo, Pa.' I sniffed. Pa was sketching some flowers.

'I hadn't noticed these before. Just smell them,' Pa said. The bean flowers were multicoloured, white, blue, yellow, pink, and the sweetest of all a strange colour, neither white nor green. Somewhere a person sneezed. 'The cats love them.' Pa went on drawing. Old X-ray and Angelique were winding and twining along the row of beans. Watching them I saw the ginger cat, then I sneezed so hard tears came to my eyes.

'Sandy's here,' I said. 'Come to pester you.'

'Oh bother! What does he want?'

'Pictures. He wants you to have another show.

'Hah!' Pa flung down his pad and stood up in a rage.

'Ma is giving him breakfast.'

'She should have given him hemlock.'

'Now Pa, don't get worked up.'

Pa sneezed. 'It's the flowers,' he said. 'I wonder what they are?'

'Beans.'

'Rubbish. Oh, well, I suppose I'd better go in. Hide this for me.' He handed me the sketch pad. 'Put it somewhere safe where he can't see it.'

'I'll put it in the hat,' I said, but he did not hear me.

'The flowers are lovely. Thank you,' I called to the empty garden. There was no answer. I peeped in on the toads among the irises. Their sides moved a little as they breathed. I left the garden, the cats staring after me, unblinking, sitting among the beans, sleepy, luxurious. I had the feeling that someone other than the cats was watching me, too.

I rolled up Pa's sketch and put it in the hat where it hung on the stand. Sandy was tucking in to eggs and bacon, talking with his mouth full, looking up at Pa who stood leaning against the wall.

'Be reasonable,' Sandy munched. 'With a tumbledown place like this you need the money. Why, half of it has no roof.'

'That doesn't matter,' I said.

Sandy gulped coffee. 'The fire damage in the hall is frightful.'

'Could have been worse,' said Pa.

'You told me when you bought it there was no light, no mains water, no proper road, but this is ridiculous.'

'We like it that way.' Pa arched his back, resting his shoulders against the wall. I could see it annoyed Sandy, who was a short man, to be looking up at Pa. 'Why don't you sit down?'

'I like standing.'

'Listen,' said Sandy, 'be reasonable. Your public wants to buy Andrew Fullers. Suppose you give me all the work you've done so far and I'll take it up to London—organize another show for you?'

'I couldn't do that.'

'But you will need the money.'

'Will I? What for?'

'You have a wife, children, your father, hangers-on.' Sandy glanced at David and Mr Bailey who sat quietly eating their breakfasts. Pa said nothing. 'You can't have much left of your windfall. You need money to keep up this establishment, such as it is.' Sandy's voice implied that the Augean stables were on a par with Haphazard.

'Hah!' Mr Bailey uttered. 'Hah!' Sandy ignored him.

'You can't have much left. You'll never have a break like that horse again.'

'Dear horse,' said Ma. 'What was it called? I forget.'

'False Start,' I said.

'Well?' Sandy looked at Pa.

'I haven't much time to paint.'

'You've had ages.'

'I've a new style. I haven't one canvas for you.'

'But you must have.'

'No must about it.' Pa's face was in shadow at the top of his six-feet-four. 'Anyway, nobody's having what I'm painting now.'

'What!' Sandy could not believe his ears. 'I come all this way, take the trouble when you don't answer my letters; a gallery laid on, all we need is the pictures. People want Andrew Fullers.'

'Then want must be their master.'

'I'm your agent.'

'You *were* my agent.'

From his seat in the window Grandpa began to laugh.

'Hear that?' he cried. 'No more pictures. No more Fullers. No more money for *you.*' Sandy looked put out. 'What did you charge him? Twenty per cent? Twenty-five? The boy is busy. Hasn't time for you. He's painting me; immortalizing his aged father while there's time. He hasn't time for you.'

'I'm only—' Sandy half rose.

'Only wasting time,' cried Grandpa gleefully. 'Isn't it time you were off?'

'Grandpa, please,' Ma protested.

'Time, time, time,' Grandpa shouted, snapping his fingers at Sandy. 'Your time is money, it's something quite else here.' He sprang up, his halo of white hair bright.

'Come on, Father. To work.' Pa pushed himself away from the wall and left the kitchen with Grandpa.

Sandy looked beseechingly at Ma. 'Can't you do something?'

She said, 'I'm sorry, Sandy, but it's over. All that bad time is over.'

'D'you mean he's stopped painting, got a block?'

'Oh no,' said Ma, 'oh no, not that. It's just—'

'What?'

'It's just that there isn't anything for you here. We'd love you to stay of course. Why don't you?'

'I've no time.' Sandy got to his feet. 'Thank you very much for breakfast but I'd better be on my way. I've no time to waste.'

'Oh, poor you.' Ma sounded sad. 'Unhappy man.'

'Perhaps I'll come later on and Andrew will have some stuff then.'

'Don't waste your time,' I said, feeling sorry for Sandy. 'You need your time, we have plenty.' As I spoke I wondered what I was talking about, what I meant.

'Well,' Ma spoke quietly. 'Lisa and Josh will see you back to your car.'

'It's broken down.'

'I daresay it will start now it's had a rest.'

'Jaguars don't need to rest. My car's not a horse.'

'Well,' Ma looked at Sandy then at Josh.
'Come on.' Josh caught Sandy's arm. 'It'll start if we push.'
We led Sandy away. As we left the house Josh took the hat from the stand. Ma called after us. 'If you see Mr Pearce ask about the Aga.'
'Okay,' we shouted as we moved off. I waved up to the window above the porch where a ginger cat sat sunning itself. Josh took off the hat with a flourish and bowed. Sandy looked up at the house. 'Who are you waving to?'
'We are just being childish,' I said, looking down at my legs in their old jeans. 'These wouldn't have fitted this morning.'
'What?' said Sandy.
'Nothing.'
'You lot are all crazy. This Haphazard dump has gone to your heads.' Sandy was vehement in his disgust and disappointment.

Chapter 22

Sandy's Jaguar stood beside the pub. It looked very grand and out of place. The church tower seemed to be rearing away from it, offended.
'It just stalled.' Sandy put his hand on the bonnet.
'Cars do here. Get in. We will push you.'
'This has been a fruitless visit.' Sandy got into the driving seat.
'Scarcity will increase the value of what Fullers there are.' Josh tried to cheer him up. Looking at Sandy I remembered the sad days in Croydon when Ma had said to Sandy, 'If he could sell just one or two it would give him hope, give him time to work without always worrying about money.'
'Come on,' I said to Josh, 'push.' We pushed. Nothing happened. 'Have you got the brakes off?' I asked.

'Of course I have. I'd better push, too.' Sandy got out and began pushing from the side, his hand on the wheel to steer.

'Half the trouble with your father's pictures *is* their scarcity,' he puffed.

'There were three hundred in the show,' I said, remembering.

'More than half have disappeared. We can't trace them.'

'How's that?' Josh was getting red in the face from exertion.

'Some clever dick cornered the market.' Sandy stopped pushing. 'She's not going to move.'

'Oh yes she is. Get in,' I said, taking the hat off Josh's head and putting it on the Jaguar's bonnet. 'Try the starter.'

Sandy tried. The noble engine purred into life.

'There.' I stood beside him looking in. Josh retrieved the hat. 'Off you go.'

'Thank you.' Sandy suddenly looked happier. 'Thank you very much. I'm glad I came in spite of everything.'

'Glad? Why?'

'This is a magical place, so unexpected. I shall come again some day.'

We stood in the road waving. 'I think I'd better take the hat home. Just imagine if he'd driven off with it on the bonnet!' Josh held the hat against his chest.

'Here comes David,' I said, 'with Bogus.' We stood waiting for them.

'Your ma thought I'd better come up as Mr Pearce will be behind the bar, and you are too young to go into the pub.'

'I don't know that I am.' I remembered myself that morning in the mirror. Josh drifted away, carrying the hat. 'Anyway, I'd like a drink,' I said. 'No law against that.'

'I'll bring you a glass of wine.' David went into the pub, leaving me under the oak tree. I could hear the church clock above me and swallows whistling. The inn sign creaked. David brought me a glass of wine. He was followed by Mr Pearce.

'Morning,' said Mr Pearce. 'Hullo, Rags, how's tricks

then?' Bogus thumped his tail. Mr Pearce patted him. 'Getting settled in then?' Mr Pearce sat beside me. He wore corduroy trousers tied under the knee with string, and a red handkerchief round his neck. He smelt of hay, sweat and beer. 'You like it at Coldharbour then? Getting settled in?'

'Yes, we love it. We are all very happy.'

'All?'

'Well, Edward and Victoria left.'

'They'd have to, wouldn't they? It was young Arnold. Couldn't stay after that, could they?'

'After what?' I said. 'After what?'

'David here says your ma is interested in an Aga.' Mr Pearce ignored my question.

'Yes, she'd like one please. She wants to keep the range though. What happened to Arnold, Mr Pearce?'

'Young Arnold?' Mr Pearce glanced briefly over his shoulder at the tombstones dancing their ballet. 'Tell your ma I'll bring the Aga tomorrow. She'd like a red one I take it? Look nice with all the copper.'

'When did young Arnold die?' I asked doggedly.

'Before you was born I should say. Rags was quite a puppy.' Mr Pearce fondled Bogus's ears. '*Nearly* died.'

'Did he recover?'

Mr Pearce looked vague. 'Time you went home. Tell her I'll bring the Aga.' The scent of beer receded as he went back to the pub.

David took the wine glass from my hand and put it on the step of the pub. 'Come on.' He took my hand.

We walked in silence through the wood, across the grass to the house, the midday sun in our eyes. The person at the window was watching. We both waved. The person waved back.

'It's difficult to see in this sunlight,' I said.

'In any light,' said David.

'Did you notice Mr Pearce's clothes, David? Weren't they a bit—'

'My credulity is elastic,' he said.

Chapter 23

I climbed the hill behind the house. I wanted to test what Josh had said about the house not being there when he looked down from the hill. I wore the hat.

The way led up through beech woods. The trees towered above, grey boles, branches springing out, blocking the sky; here and there red and yellow fungus. The air under the trees was still. Above, the breeze rustled the leaves. The path zigzagged uphill. I was soon out of sight of the house. I felt I remembered the way and reproached myself for being fanciful.

A fox crossing a clearing paused and looked at me, its eyes brightly interrogating. I reached the top of the hill, coming out on to a grassy space. I climbed on a rock and looked around. Unafraid of me, rabbits nibbled grass, sat up, washed their ears, lolloped to and fro showing white scuts. High up a buzzard screamed. I watched it circling on the warm thermals. It was joined by its mate. They circled the top of the hill until some rooks flew up to mob them, then drifted away. I looked down over the wood to the valley. Haphazard was reassuringly there below me.

I could see everything in miniature. In the walled garden Mr Bailey was sitting by the iris clump. The rows of fruit and vegetables criss-crossed the garden, each a different shade of green except for the row of Victoria's beans. The colours of the flowers fused like a rainbow. I saw my mother join Mr Bailey. She offered something, which he refused. I guessed that she had remembered to pay him for the taxi she had had to take from St James's Square the day we bought Haphazard. It seemed an infinity ago. Grandpa came briskly down the steps of Pa's loft. The sun shone directly on his head. I craned forward to see. Was his head bald or was it covered with iron-grey hair? Where the stream ran through the wood I could see the pool, Josh and David swimming. Bogus lolled against the front door. Old X-ray and Angelique basked at the kitchen window; smoke drifted gently up from the chimneys. I watched it, trying to see the exact point where the smoke became invisible. My eyes travelled up with it. Even here on top of the hill I had to raise my head. Unable to locate the invisible point, I looked down. Gone was the house. Gone my mother. Gone the kitchen garden, the cats, Grandpa, Mr Bailey, Bogus—gone Josh and David, only an open grass clearing below.

I felt that rare sensation of blood draining from my face. I shut my eyes, held my breath, listened, hoped. The buzzards screamed to each other. I kept my eyes shut. I was afraid. They had all gone, become as invisible as the man who tilled the garden, lit the fires, brought the vegetables, planted beans. Was I, too, invisible or was I sitting here on a rock on top of a hill with rabbits nibbling among harebells?

I whispered, 'Haphazard, come back. When I first saw you in horrible Heath's waiting-room I knew we belonged to you. Haphazard, don't go away.'

I pressed my fingers to my eyes, not daring to look. Were my fingers the ones I had seen that morning in the mirror, Fear was choking me, it was hard to swallow. I opened my eyes and looked at my hands. I was so frightened I could not tell whether they were mine or that girl's. Someone was watching me. I stood up.

Below in the clearing a man looked up at me. He wore the hat.

But I was wearing the hat! I let out a yell from bursting lungs in dry-throated terror. Eerily my cry echoed downhill through the trees.

The man lifted his arms and waved the hat. He called my name, 'Lisa-a-a-'

Trembling, I took off the hat, held it against my chest. I stared down at the man looking up at me.

A wind had risen, whisking my hair across my face. I brushed it away with angry fingers. The man was less distinct as I stared down, trying to see his face. His figure became hazy. I began to see the outlines of the house behind him, Mr Bailey alone now in the garden, Ma and Pa strolling out of the house, holding hands, Grandpa reading a newspaper. A newspaper! We had no newspapers, we had not seen a newspaper since we left London. Grandpa turned a page, giving the newspaper a shake. I could read the headlines.

'Tragedy of octogenarian in top floor flat. Mr Fuller, eighty-two, in his Bloomsbury home due for demolition —' Grandpa flipped over another page. I could see no more. I tried to move but I couldn't. I struggled to get the hat on. The colours of the house and garden below were vivid. I could see the scarlet fruit of the irises, the many-coloured beans, Grandpa's white halo of hair, his polished head, the brilliant fur of the cats, the grass, Ma's teeth flashing as she laughed with Pa. The stranger had gone. I stood up. A hawk swooped like a bullet to snatch a mouse from the grass. I began to run, racing down through the trees, scrambling, jumping, tearing downhill to erupt beside my parents who were sitting, chatting idly.

'Hullo.' Pa looked up. 'Heavens, you look hot.'

'What have you been doing? You look dishevelled.' Ma held her hand to shade her eyes.

'I was looking down from the top. I—er—ran back when I saw you.' I sat down to get my breath, to still my trembling legs.

'That's nice,' said Ma.

'I thought I saw Grandpa reading a newspaper.'

Ma and Pa burst out laughing.

'A paper! Here! A *newspaper*! You were dreaming.'

'No papers,' said Ma.

'No television,' said Pa.

'No noise, no harassment, no fuss,' said Ma. 'No aggro.'

'No creditors, no hurry, no bores to waste one's time,' said Pa.

'There was Sandy,' I reminded him.

'Oh, the poor fellow,' exclaimed Pa cheerfully. 'Came all that way with expectations only to go back empty-handed.'

'Not a sausage,' I said, feeling better.

'A shame really.' Ma smiled. 'Especially as you *are* painting.'

'No luck with Victoria. Couldn't catch that girl.'

'She wasn't really here to catch,' said Ma ambiguously. 'How are you getting on with your father?'

'Rather well. I am pleased so far.'

'The newspaper headline seemed to say—' I began. Then I paused. 'Tragedy' it had said. Did not 'tragedy' usually imply death?

'Newspaper headlines always "seem" but are rarely true. Anyway you couldn't have read it at that distance.' Pa idly took the hat from my head and put it on.

'Of course I couldn't,' I agreed.

'I've changed my style,' said Pa to Ma. 'I'm painting really well.'

'It's you who has changed. You are much nicer since we got here. It's affected your work.'

It had been a dream, just a bad dream. I had enjoyed it in a way. I had felt happiness with the fear.

'Time for supper.' Ma got up, holding out her hands to us. I had not realized how late it was. 'Sandy's visit was a bit—'

'Disturbing.' Pa tilted the hat. We joined Grandpa sitting with the cats.

'I saw you up on top of the hill,' he said to me. 'What can you see from there?'

'Nothing.' I remembered my desolation. 'Nothing at all.'

Grandpa coughed. 'If there's nothing to see I won't go up, though my pipes are greatly improved.'

'If they are so improved you could climb up to bed like a civilized person,' said Ma, using slight asperity.

'Do you wish to kill me?' Grandpa stared at her.

'Don't speak of death!' I exclaimed, remembering my fear.

'Hush now.' Pa spoke briskly, reassuringly. 'We forgot our manners, we forgot to wave.'

We all ran backwards until we could see the window

above the porch. We waved, and Pa doffed the hat. In the dusk the person waved behind the glass.

'He seems to have a cat.' Ma went ahead into the house.

'A marmalade cat,' said Pa.

'Ginger,' Mr Bailey corrected him.

'All right, if you say so.' Pa was amiable. 'I must admit my parent has a point. Stairs are usual. They are a convenience.'

'A catalyst,' said Mr Bailey.

'What's that?' I asked.

'Something that joins or connects things together, loosely. Stairs would connect the ground floor with your grandpa's bedroom, see?'

'Yes. Mr Bailey, I had a funny dream on top of the hill.' I felt a need to confirm.

'Dreamed you was back in Croydon?'

'That would have been a nightmare,' I exclaimed. Again I remembered Ma speaking to Sandy long ago, well before Derby Day. 'Oh, Sandy, if he could just sell *one*.' Her face had been strained, lined, worried, unhappy, old.

'What was the dream, then?' Mr Bailey enquired.

'I don't think I can tell you after all.' I remembered the man calling my name. 'It was a nice dream, really.'

'That's good. Like me putting tickets on cars and dreaming of toads was it?'

'Something like that. It was something I want.'

Chapter 24

I lay listening to the house waking. A mouse scratched under the boards, a bumblebee zoomed by. I got up and leaned out of my window, wondering whether the man two or three windows along the landing was also looking out.

Along the wall an open window enabled me to hear my parents waking. Pa yawned loudly. They laughed. I heard their door open and the sound of them going down the corridor.

From out of the wood Mr Pearce came leading a horse pulling a cart. On the cart, gleaming in the sun, was a red Aga. Ma walked out to meet Mr Pearce. I watched her. From the back anyone not knowing her age would take her for nineteen or twenty, not a woman with a son of fourteen and me, Lisa, aged eleven.

When I climbed down the ladder Mr Pearce, with David helping him, was lowering the Aga to a trolley. 'Easy now, easy.' It looked difficult.

The horse, its head turned to watch, wore blinkers. It had bright brasses on its harness. Ma stroked its nose. It mumbled her fingers with whiskery lips. 'What a magnificent colour.' Ma admired the Aga.

'I knew you'd want red. Goes nicely with the copper pots.'

'It certainly will.' Ma sounded pleased. 'Could we turn your horse loose to graze or will he go home?'

'He'll stay.' Mr Pearce unharnessed the horse who shook himself. The harness marks were dark on his light, bay coat. He smelt of sweat, and blew down his nose before starting to crop grass, mumbling among the sweet tufts with grey lips.

Mr Pearce and David began manoeuvring the stove through the front door. The trolley stuck. Mr Pearce pushed and heaved, his muscles bunched. David pulled.

'Come on, lass, youm going to like it here,' Mr Pearce addressed the Aga. 'Come on then, try.' After a while he began to wheedle. 'Just a little try. Youm being obstinate; 'tis here you belong to be.'

I climbed over the sill of the hall window, took the hat from the stand and put it on Mr Pearce's head. The trolley zoomed through the door, nearly knocking David down, and rolled sweetly along to the kitchen. I retrieved the hat, put it back on the stand and stroked the silky straw with my finger. My mother watched me.

By afternoon the Aga was installed beside the Edwardian range which Ma had blackleaded so that it shone, showing up its brass fittings. The copper kettles bubbled on the hob, thin lines of steam wavering to the ceiling.

Ma made tea while Mr Pearce stood back to admire his work.

'That's what was needed; ancient plus modern.'

'Absolutely.' Ma handed Mr Pearce his mug. 'My period.'

'Made it all nice; quite settled in.' He looked approving, then stooped to stroke Old X-ray who sat, feet together, facing the range, her eyes closed. 'Cat's happy.'

'Yes.' Ma offered more tea which was accepted, and cake.

'All happy then? Got a new bloke since I seen you, stopped to ask the way. "This Coldharbour then?".' Mr Pearce gave a fair imitation of Mr Bailey. '"I'm looking for Coldharbour," he said to my wife; a cockney type.'

'He is from London. His name is Bailey.'

'He suited here?'

'Seems very happy. He plays chess, loves the country.' Ma sat at the table looking at Mr Pearce amiably. 'He's settled.'

'Your husband fixed up?'

'Very busy painting.'

'Father-in-law?'

'My husband is painting his portrait.'

Mr Pearce swallowed some tea, then said casually, 'Those two with young Arnold now—'

'They left. I told you,' I said. 'Don't you remember?'

'Ah yes, so you did. Couldn't have stayed could they? Bit of an error that was. A slip-up somewhere after what happened before.'

'Mr Pearce.' Ma looked him in the eye. 'Why are there no children in Coldharbour?'

'Well—' Mr Pearce looked shifty.

'Well, what?' Ma asked briskly.

'We don't get many.' Mr Pearce was barely audible. 'Not these days. He was the last, young Arnold.' Mr Pearce spoke so quietly I barely heard him. Ma looked strangely at him.

'I thought as much. What about Josh and Lisa?'

'Oh they belong. They always belonged. You must have known that.'

Ma let out her breath in a long sigh and nodded at Mr Pearce.

'Ah, just look at that!' Mr Pearce exclaimed suddenly, his hearty self pointing at Angelique stepping proudly into the kitchen carrying a white mouse.

'Mouse!' David upset his tea and leapt at Angelique who let him take Mouse from her. 'Unhurt,' he said, relieved, 'but she's pregnant.' Mouse indeed looked that way.

'Your mouse?' Mr Pearce looked interested.

'She was to have had experiments done on her.'

'Looks as though she's tried one on her own. Mr Hayco liked a good, white mouse. You belong here, young David, you belong. She'll have a pretty litter; piebald they'll be.'

'She nearly didn't.' David looked furiously at Angelique who was grooming herself. 'Horrible animal! She's not like her mother.'

'Old X-ray thinks she's an elephant. She's afraid of mice,' Ma explained. 'Put Mouse somewhere safe, David, in a box or something. Tell us more about Mr Hayco, Mr Pearce.'

'Nay. You can find that out for yourselves.' Mr Pearce assumed a mulish expression.

'I daresay,' said Ma lightly. 'More tea? No? The next thing we'd like you to help us with, Mr Pearce, is the stairs. My father-in-law can't get up and down the ladder. Didn't you say there were stairs? That Mr Hayco had some made?'

The blood drained from Mr Pearce's face then rushed back until he was purple with anger. He spoke harshly. 'I did not say anything about stairs.'

'You implied.' Ma stood her ground.

'I did not. 'Tis wrong to say so. I ain't got no power over stairs, I tell you. 'Tis up to you.'

Ma held her ground. 'I had rather gathered there had been some made, or planned.'

'I didn't say so.'

'Not in so many words. But you must admit we need stairs.'

'What's wrong with the back stairs then? I'll mend the few unsteady treads. I'll do that tomorrow.'

'And the others? Up to us you say?'

'No hurry.'

'But Mr Pearce—'

Mr Pearce crashed his fist on the table. 'I tell you there's no hurry, none at all.'

'I see nothing unusual in our having front stairs.' I had never heard Ma speak so forcibly. 'A spiral staircase. We'll set the figures from the van on the banister rail. It will suit Grandpa. He wants stairs. He says so.'

Mr Pearce glared at Ma, then got up and made for the door.

'I'll mend those treads.' His voice was his normal one, his rage gone. 'There's no need for haste.'

We watched him catch the horse, harness it to the cart and drive away, sitting stiff.

'What on earth made me say all that?' Ma murmured.

'About the stairs and the brass figures?'

'Yes. I must be mad. I saw them in my mind's eye quite clearly.'

'You weren't even wearing the hat,' I said.

'I see them spiralling up from the hall. The sun lights them up.' Ma made a circular movement with her finger, her eyes on her vision. This was the girl Pa had fallen in love with.

'I wonder why he says there's no hurry?' Ma's eyes focussed on me. She was herself again.

'Where were you, Ma?'

'Just then?'

'Yes.'

'Some place in my mind where that staircase is a fine place.'

Chapter 25

I followed David to the library, Mouse in his cupped hand, her pink nose sniffing out between his thumb and finger.

'I don't think she's puzzled,' I said to David's back. 'I think she knows something, my Ma.'

'It's not like her to be so tough. She was tough with Comrade Pearce.' David opened a drawer in a kneehole desk and Mouse went in cautiously.

'Are you pleased he said you belong?'

'I knew I did.' David pushed Mouse with a gentle finger. 'You'll be all right there. You can breathe through the keyhole.' He shut the drawer. 'Safe from that Angelique. Diabolic I'd call her.'

'How did you know you belong?' I asked.

'I knew it in the back of my head. That's where thoughts which aren't quite ready lurk, haven't you noticed? Your pa has them about his painting, like the job he wants to do on Victoria. Some day when he's ready he'll get that girl on canvas, beads, elbows and all. He's just not ready.'

'Ma seems ready for the stairs.'

'Comrade P. isn't. Doesn't act ready, does he? Run along. I want to read.' David picked up a book and lay down on the sofa, withdrawn. He had even forgotten Mouse. I went to the kitchen, mixed bread and milk in a saucer and brought it to Mouse. She was busy shredding paper at the back of the drawer. David did not look up.

'David,' I interrupted.

David looked up, keeping his place in the book with a finger. 'What is it?'

'David, have you noticed what's going on here?'

'What's bothering you?' He looked ready to listen.

'Somebody's watching us.'

'The gent in the window? He isn't there you know. I've looked.'

'So have I, but he still waves, and we all wave now. It's only polite.'

'There isn't a room there.'

'I can't find it but it is there. I am certain.'

'If you say so. What else?'

'No papers, no post, no television, no telephone.'

'No communications—I like it. Suits me. Suits Mouse.'

'Somebody works in the garden. Somebody brings in vegetables.'

'Somebody also brings in groceries, eggs, milk and meat, sees to the fires, does the work, cleans the house. I have noticed.' Patiently.

'Ma cooks.'

'It's token cookery. She cooks when she wants to, she does a sort of family cooking act. Have you seen her wash up?'

'No, not often. I can't remember.'

'Suits me. I hate chores. I like to read.'

I took the hint. 'I'll go in a minute, leave you in peace.'

'It's okay. What else?'

'Are you being watched?'

'No, not me or Mr Bailey.'

'Josh?'

'Sometimes, I think. It's possible.'

'I'm watched a lot. It's a man. He wears the hat.'

'One like it, perhaps. The house is supposed to be haunted isn't it?'

'Pa said it was a sales gimmick. The man called to me, too.'

'What's really bothering you? Didn't you answer?'

Afraid he would laugh at me, I told him how I had woken to find myself grown-up. David listened attentively and finally said, 'Um.'

'Also,' I said, since he hadn't laughed, 'Ma looks years younger than she used to. You must have noticed.'

'Country air?'

'Country air doesn't get rid of grey hair and lines. Then there is Grandpa. I have caught him several times looking about Pa's age—thick hair, David.'

'He's as bald as a coot.'

'Not always. And another thing. When we first got here

Mr Pearce wore blue jeans and drove a tractor. Now he wears corduroy trousers tied below the knee with string and drives a cart and horse.'

'So you assume before long he'll be wearing a smock, a funny hat and touching his forelock.'

I giggled.

'He well might.' David was pleased to have made me laugh. 'It's all in the mind,' he said. 'Now push off and let me read.'

'Ma is not puzzled.' It occurred to me this was indeed true.

'Nor me. Run along, do. Leave me in peace.'

'Thanks for listening, David.'

'Goodbye,' said David firmly, burying his nose in his book.

I left him. Finding Bogus in the hall I went outside.

'Bogus, I've got thoughts in the back of my head coming forward,' I said to him. He cavorted with pleasure. On the way to the wood I looked back and waved. And he, or perhaps he didn't, waved back.

I planned a visit to the post office feeling that if I could get Mrs Pearce talking she might add a bit to my puzzle.

'You are an important bit of the puzzle,' I said to Bogus who wagged in appreciation. 'Ma and Grandpa look younger than they are.' Bogus turned aside to snuff in the grass. He jerked back as a frog jumped with a plop into the ditch. I watched it swim, then let its legs trail. 'Somebody waves from that window, Bogus, we all see him.' I walked on. 'It was something pretty fishy that made Edward and Victoria leave.' Bogus was unresponsive. Drops of rain began pattering through the trees, the wind was rising, the tops of the trees began to sway. 'Something about a staircase, and cars that don't work; its ridiculous.' Bogus looked up and barked. 'And they call you "Rags"; that's ridiculous, too.' Bogus barked cheerfully, not minding the rain, not threatened by ideas, not afraid. I wished I had brought the hat with me.

Chapter 26

By the time we reached the village the rain was stinging my face. It hissed on the road, drove slanting against the headstones in the churchyard. I went into the post office, wiping the water out of my eyes.

'Good afternoon.' Mrs Pearce greeted me from behind the counter. The pearls gleamed on her bosom, pink as shrimps.

'I am afraid we are rather wet,' I apologized, as Bogus shook himself and sat down to lick his chest and stomach.

'People get wet when it rains.' Mrs Pearce gave the impression that she was imparting an erudite piece of information.

There was a stool by the counter. I hoisted myself on to it so that I perched, my eyes level with Mrs Pearce's.

'Mr Pearce brought us an Aga.'

'That's so. To suit your ma.'

'My father's agent came to see whether he had any pictures ready.'

'Went away empty-handed.' Mrs Pearce's pearls moved gently up and down her bosom.

'How did you know?'

Mrs Pearce indicated by the slightest twitch of an eyebrow that this question was a silly one.

I tried again. 'Victoria and Edward took Baby away in the bus.'

'Best way to go isn't it? Better than that hearse thing.'

'Have you seen the hearse? It's a van now.'

'It won't be needed here.'

'I'm glad to hear that.' I wondered whether Mrs Pearce ever unbent or expressed surprise.

'Nothing surprises me.' Mrs Pearce showed a mouthful of teeth, threw back her head and laughed. The pearls clattered.

'Not since 1665,' I said boldly. Mrs Pearce's teeth clicked shut. 'Where is Mr Hayco buried? Which is his stone?' I waved towards the churchyard.

'Who said he had one? Like a toffee?' Mrs Pearce took the top off a jar of toffees and offered it—a friendly gesture. I took one and began untwisting the paper.

'That'll clamp your jaws.'

'Oh,'—my mouth was open for the toffee—'are you suggesting I talk too much?'

'I'm saying it.'

'About 1665? The Plague? Mr Hayco? What else?'

'The Plague.' Mrs Pearce looked through me.

'What was it like?' I put the toffee in my mouth.

'You can read all about it in your history books.'

'But here, here in Coldharbour?' I forced out the question. Speech was possible in spite of the toffee.

Mrs Pearce waved a hand in a circling motion. 'This was a very big village, almost a town. That's why the church is so big. Nearly everyone died.' Mrs Pearce looked out through the rain at the church.

'The tower looks like a dog,' I said, prising the toffee from my teeth with a fingernail.

'He said that he called it "Guardoggod".' Mrs Pearce smiled grimly. 'Profanity really. One shouldn't laugh.'

'But you do. Was "he" Mr Hayco?'

'Might have been,' she said evasively.

'Either it was Mr Hayco or it wasn't.' I tried to appear polite, not to let exasperation sound in my voice. I fished what was left of the toffee out of my mouth and offered it to Bogus.

'Let him have one of his own.' Mrs Pearce unwrapped a toffee and handed it to Bogus. 'He's a good dog is Rags.'

'Not a guarddoggod? That's the sort of joke Grandpa makes.'

'Irreverent, too, is he?'

'I suppose that is what he is.'

'They get on well?' Mrs Pearce's eyes defied me not to know her meaning.

'I don't think they've met yet.' I felt the blood rising to

my face, my heart thumping. Had Grandpa and Mr Hayco met, did they know each other? Explosive thoughts crowded my brain. I stared at Mrs Pearce.

'Have another toffee, dear.'

Tears began to roll down my cheeks.

'There's nothing to cry about,' Mrs Pearce brought her face closer to mine, the pearls swinging towards me, 'just takes a bit of getting used to. 'Tis all natural.'

'It isn't—' I sniffed. Mrs Pearce reached for a box of tissues and handed me one. 'Blow.' I blew my nose and wiped my eyes.

'It isn't natural,' I said. 'No children, no people, cars don't work. Not a soul about. Grandpa looking young; Ma too. Bogus—'

'Rags.'

'Victoria and Edward, they had to leave.'

'Baby Arnold. 'Twas sad that.'

'And someone waves from the window.' I had not meant to let this escape me.

'He waves does he? That's good. Good afternoon, Mrs Fuller, what can I do for you?' Mrs Pearce swung into full postmistress splendour as my mother came into the shop. I felt relieved to see her as though she had snatched me back from something I was not ready for.

'Good afternoon, Mrs Pearce.' Ma smiled in a friendly way. 'Have you such a thing as a scrubbing brush and a bar of soap?'

'Found something needs cleaning?' Mrs Pearce was startled.

'Yes. The house is spotless as you know.' Ma smiled. She knew and I knew that there was no reason to suppose Mrs Pearce should know how spotless Haphazard, empty for so many years, could be. 'We've come across some—er—glass which needs careful cleaning.'

'Glass.' Mrs Pearce spoke as though Ma had said a bomb which needs defusing.

'Yes.' Ma glanced round. 'Ah, that brush will do

beautifully and this.' She picked up a bar of soap. 'How much is that?' She put a pound note on the counter. Mrs Pearce gave her change.

'Glass.' She was shaken.

'You shouldn't eat too many toffees darling; they ruin your teeth.' Ma took my hand. 'The rain has stopped. Come Lisa, come Bogus. It is kind of you to let them shelter. See you soon Mrs Pearce. Goodbye. Thank you.' Ma drew me to the door. 'We shall be late.'

'Late for what?' I ungraciously removed my hand from my mother's.

'Late for the unearthing, the unwatering. Come on.' Ma walked quickly along the road.

'The what?'

'Mr Bailey has found the stairs. They are as I imagined them.'

'Where? What stairs?' I hissed. 'Where?'

'At the bottom of the well in the kitchen garden.'

'I must have been standing on them when I was fished out. That's what I slipped on.'

'What on earth were you doing in the well?'

I explained. 'Poor toad,' said Ma. 'They don't like water except to spawn in. It was cruel of you.' She could not have made a worse reproach. 'What were you gossiping about with that old witch?'

'Is she a witch?'

'She might be.' Ma was matter of fact. 'Quite easily.'

'I was trying to find things out.'

'Did you?'

'Nothing that makes sense. Mr Hayco doesn't seem to have had a funeral. She knew Baby. How could she have?'

'I don't know, love.'

'He was rather disgusting, Ma.' I remembered the bus driving away. 'He licked the window of the bus, smeared it with his goo.'

'You were a baby once and licked all sorts of things; babies do.'

Ma was hurrying. When we reached the wood she began to run. I was hard put to it to keep up with her. 'Not all of them particularly nice, either.' I let this comment pass, it being as unlike my ma to be unkind as it was for her to run so fast, besides which I was bewildered to notice she was outdistancing me. She shot out of the wood, across the grass and round the corner of the house. I caught up with her in the garden.

Grandpa, Pa, Josh, David and Ma were round the well, leaning over the parapet, their bottoms forming a ring. I could hear Mr Bailey's voice booming up from the well.

'They're here, all of them, I can count them: stacked but hard to shift.'

'How on earth did he find them?' I, too, leaned over the parapet. Mr Bailey stood in the water at the foot of a ladder.

'He was poking about after toads,' Josh murmured, 'and he slipped.'

'He heaved up one bit but it fell back. Your pa is sure it's part of a glass stair,' David whispered in my ear. As David spoke Mr Bailey climbed up the ladder, then, like the rest of us, leaned over and stared into the enigmatic water, a dark mirror reflecting our faces.

As we leaned there was a flash of lightning and a crash of thunder. The rain came again, stinging our necks, lashing our shoulders.

'Indoors,' Ma shouted. 'Indoors all of you; it's dangerous.'

We followed her into the house to gather wetly round the kitchen range which Ma raked until the coals glowed, casting a red light on our faces.

'We must wait.' Ma looked up at Pa standing so tall I could not see his face. He took off the hat, shook it free of rain and laid it on the kitchen table.

The storm battered the house. The wind howled like a pack of demon wolves wailing round corners, yowling in the chimney, gusting, snuffing, grunting against the doors, thundering down from the hills across to the wood where, roaring angrily through the trees, it boomed like the sea in winter. Nobody spoke. We stood facing the fire, our backs to the storm. Old X-ray and Angelique pressed close to Grandpa, the hair on their backs raised, tails twitching. Bogus pressed his nose into my mother's hand. She stroked his muzzle with nervous fingers. Mr Bailey, standing further from the fire than the rest of us, pulled open the flap of his pocket and peered in. He took out a sizeable slow-worm and held it towards me. As I stroked its smooth length it curled, wrapping its pale brown body round his wrist.

We listened, alert, afraid, uncertain. My parents were holding hands, like children. I put mine in Grandpa's; his bony fingers closed over mine. David looked about him nervously then left us to return carrying the drawer with Mouse in it. Now we were all there, all our company. The wind abated slowly, still making angry gusts. We could hear the rain separate from the wind, drumming on the cobbles in the yard, water gushing down the gutters. It became possible to hear sounds in the house, coal shifting in the grate. The wind died suddenly, the clouds parted and the moon came out. We must have stood there a long time. In the village the church clock was striking, and in the house a clock whirred and began to strike.

Ma sighed. 'There are no clocks in the house,' she said.

'But I've heard them,' I said.

'But not seen them.'

Pa picked up the hat and put it on.

'Time was angry,' I said, not knowing why I said it or whether it was true.

'Come on all of you. Coast's clear. All's well,' Pa said.

We followed him to the well. Around the valley, disturbed by the storm, rooks circled by the light of the moon to find their roosting places, cawing raucously. Pa lowered himself over the parapet. 'Oops, it's cold!'

Chapter 27

Pa stepped off the ladder into the dark water standing up to his waist where I had stood up to my neck. He tipped the hat to the back of his head and leant down carefully.

'We shall need ropes.'

David and Josh went to find some. Pa came up to sit on the parapet, his legs hanging down. We stood round him in silence listening to the drip of water from his jeans. He began to sing quietly, 'Long ago and far away -'

'No hurry now.' Ma leant beside him. 'Look at the people over there dancing.'

'I see nobody.' Pa's eyes followed her pointing finger.

'Nobody,' I said. 'No dancers.'

'Mrs Pearce is among them. I know her by her pearls. I hadn't realized she was so young.'

'Dreams,' grunted Grandpa. 'Stuff.'

'People in dreams are often far more real than in life, especially as you grow old.'

Grandpa looked in the direction Ma had pointed, his bald head gleaming by the light of the moon, framed by the frill of white hair. 'What I see,' he said, 'are sheep and a shepherd and his dog.'

I looked towards the wood but couldn't see anything.

'Long ago and far away,' sang Pa. 'Ah, here come the boys.' Josh and David arrived carrying ropes.

'These do?'

'I think so.' Pa lowered himself down the well. 'When I've got the rope round the first step I'll say "Haul" and you pull up gently.'

We waited as he fumbled in the dark water. He had stopped singing, and muttered to himself.

Ma went to the house and returned carrying a candelabrum, all the candles lit, the flames steady.

'They had their say, then gave up.' Grandpa eyed the candles.

'Who?' I asked.

'The elements. Some call them the Furies.'
'The elements don't speak,' I said.
'Then you cannot have listened, little fool.'

I felt huffy looking at his craggy face where age had carved clefts and folds on cheeks and jaws, pleating the skin round his lips and neck. He had the appearance of a tortoise, quite unlike the man I had seen Pa painting, a man with bold eyes, large nose and iron-grey hair.

'I saw you though,' I whispered. 'I saw you when Pa was painting you.'

'Yes,' said Grandpa. 'In my prime.'

'Haul!' Pa shouted from below. 'Haul!'

David, Mr Bailey and Josh hauled while Ma guided the rope. Bogus peered over the edge, the cats looked down, ears alert, paws neat. Up from the well came a wedge, heavy, dripping.

'Careful, it's slimy.'

The first find was laid reverently on the soft earth. 'Don't let it spoil the plants!' I cried.

'It's just earth,' said Ma. She wiped the slab free of mud with her hand. 'It's glass all right, it needs a good scrub.' We all looked, standing round as she held up the candelabrum.

'Hey, I'm not getting any warmer down here.' Pa's teeth were chattering. We turned back to work.

Twenty-five slabs came up, giving little resistance. The candles grew short and the moon sank. I counted the slabs laid on the vegetable beds, narrowly triangular like the petals of a sunflower, forming a circle round the well. I stood alone as the others helped Pa climb, exhausted, up the ladder. From somewhere nearby I heard a throat cleared, then a laugh.

'I hope we are not intruding,' I said to the invisible person who did not reply. This time I was not afraid. Pa stretched aching limbs, his dripping arms reaching up to the sky. 'You look like a scarecrow,' said Ma. 'Come indoors before you catch your death.'

'He catches you.' Pa put his arm round Ma's shoulders. They went into the house. Pa hung the hat on its stand.

'Maybe some time we shall also find the banisters and the central pole, or whatever it's called.'

'The sun's rising,' called Josh. We all turned and looked from the doorway.

'The music's stopping,' David murmured. Faintly, from the far end of the house, I heard the last bars of a dance. I stood still trying to hear the music. My family talked and laughed in the kitchen, a robin sang suddenly loud from a lilac bush.

'Always up first.' Mr Bailey was beside me. He took the slow-worm from his pocket and put it down. It slid away into the Mediterranean daisies.

'Come and see Mouse's mice,' David called. 'Come quickly.'

'No need to 'urry.' Mr Bailey was ahead of me. 'They won't push off until they can see. Oh my,' he said peering into the drawer held open by David, 'you 'ave to be a real animal lover to like that lot—ugh!'

'They'll be very elegant.' David was defensive. The infant mice reached their puny paws towards Mouse.

'Ma said she would have Supermice,' I said.

'Quite right,' granted Mr Bailey. He put out his finger to stroke Mouse who bit him sharply. 'Can't call that no dream.' He sucked the injury. 'I didn't see no dancing nor hear no music but I feel yer bite. You're a good mother I'd say, got the right idea—that there X-ray ain't going to care for this lot.'

Chapter 28

Ma made Pa change into dry clothes while she got breakfast. Josh and I laid the table, David stoked the fires. Grandpa and Mr Bailey sat side by side in the window seat, their backs to the light. They looked tired. Neither spoke. When we were all sitting at the table, Ma looked round at us.

'Will you all listen a moment.' The sound of munching stopped.

'I just want to say—' She sounded nervous. 'I just have to tell you that before anybody does anything to those glass stairs we must all get some sleep.' There was a babble of protest.

'I mean it.' Ma reached for the hat on the table behind her and put it on. 'If from carelessness due to tiredness we crack or break a glass tread we can never replace it. So sleep is an order.'

'Order! Giving me orders are you?' Grandpa was angry.

'Yes.' From beneath the hat's brim Ma's eyes flashed.

'At my age! Accusing me of senility! At my age!'

'The reverse.'

'An infantile geriatric?'

'Not exactly.'

'What do you mean by that?'

'You know as well as I do.' Ma quelled him. 'Age is a rather dodgy subject, let's not discuss it. We must get some sleep. The stairs won't disappear.'

'Somebody should guard them.' Pa sounded exhausted.

'No need. Everyone to bed, please. Lisa can help me to clear breakfast, then we'll go to bed, too.'

They trailed away grumbling. Ma and I stacked the plates and washed up without discussion. We felt we had to. 'Nobody knows they are there. Stop worrying, Lisa.' Ma passed me a plate to dry.

'The gardener does.'

'Was he watching us?'

'Yes, if it *is* the gardener.'

'Well.' Ma rinsed the sink. 'Let's take a look before we

sleep. We can shut the garden doors; that should satisfy you.' We walked to the walled garden. Ma still wore the hat. Bogus and the cats came with us, nosing at the door. Ma pushed it open. The slabs of glass, drying in the sun, lay splayed round the well. All was quiet.

'No gardener,' said Ma.

'I've never seen him, only heard,' I said, looking at the neat rows of vegetables, the orderly fruit. 'This is where the toads live.' I showed Ma the irises. Ma peered down. 'Dear things.'

'This is where he's planted Victoria's beans.' I showed Ma the glorious, multicoloured flowers.

'Victoria's beans? What do you mean?'

I told Ma.

'Well,' she exclaimed, 'I call that going too far. Poor Victoria, poor girl, she was so upset.'

'But she got away, she and Edward, Baby, too.'

'What makes you say that?' Ma was sharp.

'I don't know,' I said, ' I really don't. Sandy got away as well. They all *wanted* to. They didn't really belong here.'

'Oh yes, I see that. Perhaps they will come back later on. Come on, bed for both of us.' We bolted the door and walked round to the front of the house. I looked up at the window above the porch and so did Ma.

'Not there this morning,' she said, hanging up the hat.

'I didn't know until yesterday you saw him, too,' I said.

'We all do. He's a friend.'

'Does he wave and beckon?'

'He waves,' she said dryly and sent me to bed up the back stairs.

I heard music somewhere, whether in the house or in my head I did not know but I danced and twirled along the passage to my room, dreaming that I wore full skirts which swung out as I danced through the sunbeams. I cast off my clothes and went to draw the curtains. As I looked out I saw a circle on the grass where many people had trod. I scrambled into bed, wishing I had seen them dance, joined them perhaps, got to know them, made friends.

In my sleep I dreamed I was in bed at Haphazard, that it was time to get up, but I thought in my dream, I *am* in bed and it can't be time to get up. I am tired. Ma has just sent me to bed even though it is daylight. I turned my face away from the light so that I could sleep. I heard someone come in and draw the curtains. The sun shone into my room. The rooks were cawing in the wood as they do in early autumn when they fly round oaks burdened with acorns, pecking at them, springing about the branches, cawing, 'Acorns, caw, what shall we do? Caw. Winter is near—here—caw.' A scratching and whining. I got up to let Bogus in. I was drugged with sleep. Back in bed I pulled the bedclothes round my head. Bogus did not settle as usual, laying his head beside me, pushing his body against me for warmth. He pawed at the bedclothes, scraping them off my face. I flung out an arm to hold his neck, to keep him quiet. He sat up. I could feel his tail waving, little gusts of air round my face. He sat, ears pricked, listening. Listening to what? I sat up and listened, too.

Down the passage to my room someone was walking. Who? I knew all my family's footsteps. These steps were shorter than Grandpa's but firmer. They did not diminish as they would have done if someone were just passing my door. Whoever it was was marking time. Marking time? Whoever it was gave a cough, cleared his throat. 'I am asleep. I am dreaming. This is horrible. I must wake up.' I held my head in my hands shaking it from side to side. Bogus jumped off the bed and ran to the door, wagging his tail. 'I am asleep. I am dreaming,' I assured myself out loud as I watched the handle of the door turn. 'I am afraid. I must forget this. It isn't happening—I must forget,' I shouted out loud in panic. 'I *will* forget.'

'Rags?' A voice called. Bogus scratched to get out.

'Bogus,' I whispered. 'I am dreaming. Come back.'

Bogus clawed at the door, lying on his side digging at the

door, making throaty, gasping noises. The footsteps stopped.

'Rags?' said a man's voice.

'Bogus, oh Bogus, don't go. *Please*.'

I was out of bed, running to hold Bogus back. Terror such as I had never experienced, or will again, exploded. Bogus wriggled through the door and leapt up, overcome with joy.

'There boy, there. Steady, my beauty, steady. It's been a long time for me, too.'

Bursting through the door Bogus had kicked it back at me so that I sat back abruptly, defenceless, looking up.

'Hullo, Lisa.' Mr Hayco held out a hand to help me to my feet.

'I am asleep, I am dreaming,' I said through clenched teeth. 'I want to wake up. I want to wake up at once. I shall forget this.'

'Not this time.' Mr Hayco wore a Panama hat. 'This one is mine.' He smiled. My heart thumped. 'Heart thumping?' he was watching me as he gentled Bogus.

'Yes,' I whispered. I began to cry, tears splashing down the front of my nightdress. 'I'm asleep,' I said, a grain of spirit returning.

'Then it's time you woke up.'

'Time—' I whispered. Then, not knowing why, I said aloud, 'I hate time.'

'Nothing to hate. Time is a bit askew that's all.' Mr Hayco sounded perfectly reasonable.

'Why?' My heart was thumping less. Bogus was calming down.

'I think I can explain it.' Mr Hayco lifted his hat and smoothed his thick white hair before replacing it on his head. 'Though I'm not a scientist, Lisa.'

'How do you know my name?'

'I do. I always have.'

'You call Bogus "Rags".'

'You call Rags "Bogus".'

'I hadn't thought of it that way.'

'So I noticed.' Mr Hayco looked amused. 'To me he is "Rags", to you "Bogus"—excellent name, wish I'd thought of it myself, but at that time—'

'What time?'

'The time when he was a puppy, neither particularly ragged or bogus.'

I was silent. Mr Hayco said, 'I am trying to stop you being frightened.'

'I'm not frightened.'

'Oh, but you are.'

'No.' I got to my feet.

'Well, be that as it may. Have you had anything to do with clocks?'

'Certainly not.'

'Well, you might have, you might have seen your elders winding them even though you are not allowed to touch them yourself.'

'Of course I've seen them being wound.'

'Well then,' he said. 'Seen a grandfather clock wound?'

'Yes, of course I have.'

'Seen what happens if the weights are taken off?'

'Yes,' I said, 'it goes mad, the pendulum races.'

'That's right. I call it askew, an agreeable word, askew.'

'Perhaps it is.'

'Don't be so grudging.' Mr Hayco laughed wheezily. 'It's a lovely word—askew—positively Shakespearean. D'you like Shakespeare?'

'Don't know much of it.' I was feeling better.

'Well, Lisa, that's it. That's just what it is.'

'What is what?' I was no longer afraid.

'That's better,' Mr Hayco said easily, 'you're feeling all right now, so stop being pert and take in the fact that here at Haphazard time is askew.'

'It's been askew ever since Pa bought that hat,' I said.

'I bought mine in 1949,' said Mr Hayco. 'At that time I thought it extravagant.'

'Time,' I said irritated. 'What has time, askew as you call it, what has it to do with hats?'

'Hats are timeless, ours are anyway. Now to time. Your grandfather might call it an element. We live in it we suppose—'

'And it's gone funny like a grandfather clock with the weights off?'

'Round here it has—round Coldharbour.' We were strolling down the passage, he in his hat, I in my nightdress, Bogus between us.

'Josh would call it a Time Warp,' I said, inspired.

'Ugly expression.' Mr Hayco frowned. 'I have something to show you.' He took my hand.

We were in the passage along which I had danced to bed. The window at the far end let in shafts of sun in which fluttered a butterfly.

'It can get out.' Mr Hayco followed my gaze.

'Josh and I let one out of the church.'

'Commendable. Geraldine thinks they are the souls of the dead aspiring to heaven.'

'How soppy. Who is Geraldine?'

'Geraldine Pearce at the post office. You have met her.'

'Geraldine.' I rolled the name round my tongue, spinning it out.

'Yes, it's unsuitable.' Mr Hayco turned the handle of a door. 'Come in here,' he said. 'This is my room. Step inside.'

Chapter 29

I walked across the room to the window. It was immediately above the porch.

'You wave from here?'

'Yes, and I beckon.'

There was an armchair by the window. In it, curled up in a ball, a marmalade cat. 'This is Gingerpop.' Mr Hayco picked up the cat and laid him, still curled up, on another chair. 'Night-time is his time, he hasn't much use for the daytime.'

'Is his time askew?'

'Difficult to tell with cats—think of Old X-ray and Angelique.'

'Do you know them?'

'Of course. Now sit and watch time passing.' Mr Hayco pulled up a chair for me. 'Are you cold?' He wrapped a shawl round my shoulders.'Look out of the window, Lisa.'

At first all I could see was the grass between the house and the wood, the soft, yellow-green of late summer. As I grew used to the view I saw the sheep Grandpa had remarked on. 'I see sheep, a shepherd and his dog.'

'A relative of Rags, a good dog.' Hearing his name, Bogus thumped his tail.

'Bogus,' I said. Bogus thumped again.

'Don't quibble. Keep still and watch.'

From the wood drove Mr Pearce in his lorry, jolting across the grass. He waved up at the window. Mr Hayco waved back.

'He brought the Aga in a cart,' I said, 'though the first time he came it was in the lorry.'

'He finds lorry-time more exciting. It's a matter of taste. He's not like his wife.'

'What is her time?'

'Haven't you guessed?'

I tried to guess at Mrs Pearce's time. '1665? The year of the Plague?'

'Yes. She's come on, of course—had to—but she harks back. Some people love disaster.'

As I thought of Mrs Pearce I saw unhappy people, frightened, sick. I saw the village as we had first seen it when we arrived in the van, when Josh had exclaimed at his first view of the house.

'How sad,' I said, watching the people creeping from their wretched little houses, collapsing in the road to die. 'Oh,' I clenched my hands together. 'How gruesome.' A cart loaded with bodies went slowly along the road. 'How terrible that time was. Did everyone die?'

'No. The Pearces escaped, and I did.'

'You?'

'Yes, me.'

'Who else? Edward and Victoria and their baby?'

'Poor young people. They fled from the Plague in London but they brought it with them. When they recovered they left the village. So did all the villagers except the Pearces.'

'No wonder they had to get away this time,' I said, not understanding what I tried to say.

'Look—' Mr Hayco chuckled. Swiftly from the wood came Sandy driving up to the house in his Jaguar. We watched him get down at the front door, ring the bell, listen, then stand back and look up at us.

'Does he see us?'

'No.'

'Why not?'

'Not time yet.'

'Time again.' I was irritated. 'Time askew I suppose '

'Yes, he's early.'

Sandy got into his Jaguar and drove away. I watched the car drive through a crowd of people who were gathering by the wood to dance round a fiddler. 'What are they dancing for?' I was not bothered that Sandy had not seen them.

'They celebrate. Sometimes it is Waterloo, sometimes Agincourt, now and again it is 1919, the Peace.'

'I like their clothes.' I held the shawl tightly round me. 'Those whirly-twirly skirts would be fun to dance in.'

'You did, you do, you shall.'

'Where shall I dance next?' I felt Mr Hayco should be humoured.

'Men like to be humoured,' said Mr Hayco. 'Come, Lisa, and see the time you shall dance in. Enough of that view.' He picked up Gingerpop. In his arms the cat yawned, showing the mauve of his mouth. I thought fleetingly of Mouse. 'Gingerpop is not the world's greatest mouser. Come along.' He took my hand in his. I looked at our hands. My hand was the hand of the girl in the mirror, his the hand of a young man. I wore a long dress with narrow waist and full skirts. I looked up at him and saw the face of the man who had called up from the valley, 'Lisa'.

Gingerpop and Bogus walked ahead, tails high. The passage widened into a gallery leading to the landing. All along the wall hung Pa's pictures. Ma in a deckchair, me doing a handstand.

'Haven't had time to hang it the right way up and now I like it as it is.' Mr Hayco was laughing at me. 'Why don't you call me by my proper name?' he asked.

'I don't know it. Are you Hayco's ghost? Shall I call you Mr Hayco?'

'Oh no. I am Haphazard Hayco of Coldharbour. My mother called me Haphazard. So must you.'

'Haphazard,' I said. It sounded right.

'Listen.' He stopped, pushing back the hat to hear better.

From the village came the sound of a band. 'Time to dance,' he said, whirling me along the gallery to the head of the stairs. 'Let's show our paces. This is our time at last. The ball is beginning.'

I looked down into the hall and gasped with delight.

Looking up at us were Grandpa with Old X-ray and Angelique; stretching from them to us a glass stair. From the floor of the hall to the ceiling above us was a glass pillar—radiating from it the treads we had found in the well. They shone like silver, they shone like gold. A spiral glass banister swept up beside them. At the first turn Death with his scythe, then the Fat Lady, then the Harlequin catching up with the Fleeing Girl. The sun shone through the windows striking sparks from the twists and turns.

'It's like a wine glass,' I cried.

'A spiral mercurial twist to be exact, but better.'

'How?'

'Watch closely.'

Indeed this stair was better than any glass I had ever seen. The central pillar and the banisters were hollow and up them came bright beetles and butterflies, a green frog and a toad. A snake slithered down, passing a black mouse moving up towards Mouse who was pattering down, her pink feet skittering, her whiskers atwitch. Driven mad, Old X-ray and Angelique and Gingerpop leapt and pounced, tearing up and down, crazed.

'What a tease!' I cried and Gingerpop stopped and sat rather grandly at the head of the stairs by Bogus.

'He sees the future.' Haphazard bent and stroked him. The cat paid no attention. 'Bit snobbish today, Gingerpop. This is a party.' The cat looked away.

'Dancing time. Come.' He took my hands in his. 'Listen to the music and dance.'

My heart was full of music, my feet moved, my skirts twirled out. I held his hands and we danced at the head of the stairs. My body swayed, my hair swung free. We were not alone. Dancing along the hall came Ma and Pa, young and loving, Josh with a girl I had never seen, though Josh seemed to know her, and David and Mr Bailey dancing, too. Suddenly, with a shout, came Grandpa, swinging up the stairs to meet a lovely woman as though he had never heard of aches, pains or wheezy pipes. She passed us running to meet him, to catch his hands and dance, waltzing up and waltzing down. She had eyes for no one but Grandpa, looking so full of love that for a moment I was embarrassed that anyone so old could inspire such feeling, until Haphazard, dancing with me, fingers snapping, feet tapping, cried,

'Silly, don't look like that. That's your grandmother,' and I cried out, 'So he *is* in his prime. Then who are you?'

'Can't you guess?'

I tried to see his face, shaded by the hat. A face I knew I had always known. He was laughing at me, watching me from under the brim.

'Won't I do? Don't you like what you see?'

'Who *are* you?'

'Haphazard.' I knew that voice. 'I've been calling you.'

'Oh, Haphazard!' I cried. 'Why was I afraid? I have known all along. Are we in love? Shall we grow old? Are we dead?'

'Of course we shall. Of course we are.' He took off the hat and let if float down to Grandpa who crammed it on as he danced with my grandmother.

'Aren't they beautiful?' Haphazard held me. 'They are not afraid, are you?'

'No I am not. Shall I wake up? Shall I forget?'

'Not this time. Dance, Lisa. I have waited so long for you.'

We danced down the stairs, our hearts full of joy, through a crowd of people: Ma and Pa, Mr and Mrs Pearce, he red-faced and jolly, she with her pearls swinging out in an iridescent arc, past people I had known and would know. We danced out along the path to the garden where Haphazard snatched up a swathe of bean flowers, swinging them into a garland to hold us together as we danced, for we are dancing still.

If you find this hard to believe, look across from the wood to Haphazard House on a fine, still night and you will hear the music and see us dancing in the lights reflected from the spiral stair.